I'm so scared . . .

"I want to get into my locker," she said.

"You don't get it, do you?" he said, leaning into her face.

"Get what?" she asked. She stared into his eyes. Show no fear, she thought.

"That you're the new kid on the block and I'm the guy who runs things around here. This is Jack's place, understand?"

"You run things around here?" she repeated. This was unbelievable.

"Yeah, and when I tell you to give me your quiz paper, you'd damned well do it." He leaned even closer to her. She could smell the burger he'd had for lunch on his breath. She took a step backward. "This is just a warning, okay? I figure I'll cut you some slack because you're new and all. But the next time, I'm not going to be so nice."

FIGHTING BACK

Cheryl Lanham

BERKLEY JAM BOOKS, NEW YORK

ABRAHAM LINCOLN HIGH SCHOOL

FIGHTING BACK

A Berkley Jam Book / published by arrangement with
the author

PRINTING HISTORY
Berkley Jam edition / August 2000

The Penguin Putnam Inc. World Wide Web site address is
http://www.penguinputnam.com

ISBN: 0-425-17606-1

BERKLEY JAM BOOKS®
Berkley Jam Books are published by The Berkley Publishing Group,
a division of Penguin Putnam Inc.,
375 Hudson Street, New York, New York 10014.
BERKLEY JAM and its logo
are trademarks belonging to Penguin Putnam Inc.

PRINTED IN THE UNITED STATES OF AMERICA

10 9 8 7 6 5 4 3 2 1

Chapter
One

Dear Diary,
Lansdale High is okay, I guess. So far the kids aren't
real friendly but I suppose I'll get used to them. More
important, I hope they get used to me and I make some
friends. I don't want to spend this year sitting on the
couch watching TV. I wish I could have spent my se-
nior year at El Toro. Okay, so I didn't have that many
friends there, but I had a few.

I know that Celia is doing the best she can and that
it was good of her to take me in and everything, but
sometimes I get so lonely. I wish I had someone my
own age to talk to. . . .

Amber Makepeace closed her diary and stared
blindly at the pale, white wall of her bedroom. She
sighed and tucked her leather-bound red diary into the
top drawer of the bedside table. It was quiet here, too

quiet, she thought. But that was to be expected when you live in a mobile home park and ninety percent of the other residents are senior citizens. She still couldn't understand why her cousin had decided to live here instead of an apartment or a condo. But Celia wasn't one for explaining herself. Actually, Amber thought, she wasn't one to talk much at all. That was part of the problem.

She swung her legs off the bed and got to her feet. Leaving her room, she went down the hall to the kitchen, opened the fridge and got out a soda. She popped the top of the can as she went outside into the hot September afternoon.

Mr. Cawber, the really, really old man who lived across from them, was weeding the flower bed in front of his double-wide trailer. He looked over his shoulder at her, took his hat off, wiped the sweat off his forehead and bobbed his chin in her direction to say hello. Amber gave him a jaunty wave and then sat down in one of the spindly lounge chairs that Celia had bought at the ninety-nine cent store. The chair wasn't very comfortable, the crisscrossed plastic bands would be digging into the back of her thighs within minutes, but she'd put up with the irritation just to be out of the house for a few minutes.

The mobile home had an awning that stretched completely across the drive, forming a nice shady spot. Celia had put out the chairs, but that was all. Most of the other residents in the park had converted this space into nice patio and barbecue areas. Her cousin didn't go in for that kind of thing, though, Amber had been the one to suggest they get the chairs.

"How was your first day at school?" a voice asked from behind her.

Amber started in surprise. Then she turned and saw their neighbor on the other side, Mrs. Bartlett. Lucy Bartlett was a trim, deeply tanned white-haired woman in her seventies. Dressed in a bright red-and-white flowered tank top and red Bermuda shorts, she was standing so far back in the shadows of her own awning that Amber hadn't noticed her.

"It was okay, I guess," Amber said. She wondered if she ought to invite Mrs. Bartlett to sit down.

"You mind if I join you?" the older woman asked cheerfully. Without waiting for a reply, she started toward Amber. "Sometimes it gets too quiet around this place. I could use some company."

"So could I," Amber agreed.

Mrs. Bartlett started to sit down and then paused. "We need something to set our drinks on," she said as she glanced around the area. Except for the two chairs, the patio was empty.

"There's some old TV trays stacked back there." Amber pointed toward the rear of the mobile home. "I could go get one of those."

"That'll do it. Here, give me your soda," Mrs. Bartlett instructed as Amber got up and she planted herself in the other chair.

A few moments later, Amber was back and unfolding the TV tray between the two chairs. She hoped her cousin wouldn't mind. She'd put the tray back when they were done.

"It's a bit dusty," Mrs Bartlett said as she put their

drinks down. "But a little dirt never killed anyone. So, tell me what you think of our town so far."

"Well." Amber picked up her soda and took a sip. She was trying to be polite. A dump? End of the universe? "I don't know. It's different." She decided to be diplomatic.

"Really?" Mrs. Bartlett stared at her over the rim of her iced tea. "How? I thought you were from Orange County? That's not all that different from here."

"It's not," Amber said quickly. "I just mean that I've never lived in a mobile home park before, that's all."

"Yeah, I guess that'd take some getting used to," Mrs. Bartlett agreed with a grin. Especially as the average age around here is eighty. You must feel like the Lone Ranger."

"It's okay," Amber said hastily. She didn't want to cause offense. "I mean, everyone's been real nice. I wasn't putting the place down or anything. . . ."

Mrs. Bartlett laughed. " Don't worry, honey, I know what you meant. This place does take getting used to. Hell, we practically roll the streets up at eight o'clock. You've only been here, what? A month?"

"Three and a half weeks," Amber muttered. She blinked hard and looked away. She wasn't going to cry. She wasn't going to give into the sick heartache that welled up in her throat and tried to choke the life out of her. It was better this way, much better. At least her mother wasn't suffering now. She wasn't in pain anymore.

"I'm sorry, honey," Mrs. Bartlett said gently. "I didn't mean to upset you. Celia told us about your mother at the residents' meeting when she announced you were coming to live here."

"You didn't upset me." Amber wiped at her eyes. "I'm fine. Really. It just hits me every now and then."

For a long moment, they sat in silence and sipped their drinks. Then Mrs. Bartlett said, "You okay, honey?"

"I'm fine," she assured the woman. She gave her a smile. "I just miss her so much. There was just the two of us. My dad died when I was three so Mom and I were always close."

"How long was she sick?"

"Two years," Amber replied. "I took care of her. I mean, I had help and everything. A nurse came in every day. But mainly it was just me and Mom." That was one of the reasons Amber didn't have too many friends even at her old high school. She'd known her mother was dying. She'd chosen to spend her free time taking care of her. That didn't leave much time for socializing. A couple of her old friends from junior high had hung in there with her but they'd been busy with their own lives. Amber couldn't blame them for not coming around more often. But they'd been there for her. Janice especially had always called and kept her up on all the hot gossip around school.

"Sounds like you did a good job of taking care of her," Mrs. Bartlett said softly. "She was lucky to have you."

"No," Amber replied quietly, "I was lucky to have her."

"Well said, child." She sat her glass down on the tray. "I hope you'll like it here once you get to know the place a little better. It's a good place to live, even if there are a lot of old farts around."

"It's nice," Amber protested. "I mean, I'm sure I'll get to like it; it's just that I don't know anyone here yet."

"You know your cousin."

Amber shook her head. "Not really. I knew she existed, but I'd only met her once or twice before Mom's funeral. I was stunned to find out that she was my guardian." She'd been shocked to her core when Mr. Lindstrom, their family lawyer, told her that Celia Brockton had been named in her mother's will as Amber's guardian. "But when I think about it, there wasn't a whole lot of choice. I don't have very many relatives."

"You're lucky," Mrs. Bartlett said tartly. "I've got a whole slew of 'em and between you, me and the fence post, I don't like most of 'em."

"Do they live around here?" Amber asked. She wondered if Mrs. Bartlett understood how scary it was to be so alone in the world. Except for Celia, there wasn't anyone who really cared if Amber lived or died.

"My son, Sebastian, lives up in Hillview Estates." She pointed toward the mountains that surrounded the town. "Don't see him much, he's too busy making money to have much time for me. But I see a lot of my daughter-in-law and my grandson. He went to Lansdale High."

"When did he graduate?" Amber asked.

"In June. He goes to Lansdale Junior College now. That really ticked Sebastian off. He wanted Chris to go to USC. But Marta, that's my daughter-in-law, she's got arthritis pretty bad in her hips and Chris stayed home to help her out. Told his dad he could wait a couple of years before goin' off to a four-year school. Told him he wanted to work while he went to junior college and save up some money of his own. He's a real good kid. Thoughtful, you know. Course he and his dad lock horns often enough. Sebastian's an awful snob, even if I say so myself. He's always onto Marta and Chris about lifestyles and social standards. I expect that's another reason Chris stays, he doesn't want to leave his mom there on her own. Marta's always trying to get me to come live with them, but Sebastian's such a control freak, I knew it wouldn't work. I like havin' my own place."

"Yeah," Amber agreed, "I know what you mean." She clamped her mouth shut to keep from saying anything else. Living with her cousin was like living at a hotel. Celia hadn't even bothered to put any pictures on the walls.

Mrs. Bartlett took a sip of her iced tea. "I expect you're a little lonely, aren't you? Your cousin's gone an awful lot of the time."

Amber looked down at her feet. "It does get lonely," she finally admitted.

"That'll change quick enough. Once you get involved in school, you'll make all kinds of friends."

"I hope so, Mrs. Bartlett," Amber said. "I really hope so."

Amber spent the evening alone. Just like she'd spent all the other evenings since she'd moved in with her cousin. She knew she ought to be getting used to it, but she wasn't. She was just lonely and sad and miserable.

She didn't have much homework, but she was so bored, she went ahead and finished her entire history chapter. At nine, she took her bath and put on her nightgown then wandered out into the living room to find a book or a magazine. She was halfway across the living room when she heard a key in the front door. A second later, Celia Brockton, her cousin, stepped inside.

"I didn't expect you home so early," Amber said.

Celia shrugged. She was a tall blonde woman with a thin, pale face, high cheekbones and deep-set, light blue eyes. She had on a short black skirt, a pale pink tank top and three-inch pink-and-black heels. "Dale doesn't get off work till ten so I thought I'd pop home and clean up a little."

Amber nodded. She'd forgotten this was Celia's evening to work late at the hospital. She was never sure what to say to her cousin. Celia wasn't the warmest person on the face of the earth. "Uh, how was work?"

Again, Celia shrugged. She tossed her hot-pink handbag onto the black-and-gold plaid couch. "There wasn't too much blood or gore tonight," she said. "Just a dislocated shoulder and a couple of broken bones."

Celia was a receptionist at the Lansdale Memorial Hospital emergency room. "How was school? Did you find all your classes and everything?"

"It was fine."

"Good." She started toward the bathroom. "I'm

going to take a quick shower. It Dale calls tell him I'll meet him at the Bolero."

Dale was Celia's boyfriend. He was a half-owner of an auto body shop. "Okay," Amber muttered as she watched her cousin disappear down the hall. She felt tears well up in her eyes and she blinked hard. She wouldn't cry. She wouldn't act like a baby because she was lonely. Her cousin had a right to her own life. She'd get through this. She'd make friends or whatever she had to do, and if she couldn't make any friends she'd move back to Orange County as soon as she graduated in June.

She swiped at her eyes and continued her interrupted journey to the bookcase by the couch. Kneeling down, she grabbed a paperback mystery off the top shelf and got up. She'd read until she fell asleep. Maybe tomorrow she'd have a better day. Maybe she'd meet someone nice at school.

But she didn't meet anyone, really. The other kids already had their friends and even though no one was mean or anything, no one went out of their way to befriend her either. By the end of the week, Amber had reconciled herself to being alone. Her senior year wasn't going to be any better than the other years she'd spent in high school.

She took the bus by herself from the stop outside the park entrance every morning and every afternoon. Most of the other kids either walked or had rides. She ate lunch by herself every day in a secluded spot on the quad; most everyone else ate in groups in the cafeteria or left campus to eat at one of the fast-food joints surrounding the school.

The one advantage to being on her own was that she had plenty of time to study. She was way ahead in all her classes. So far ahead, that it didn't bother her when Mr. Powers announced a pop quiz in her history class. She was probably the only one it didn't bother, though, because there was a chorus of moans from the rest of the class.

The teacher ignored their whining. "Take out a sheet of paper and number one to fifteen."

"Hey, Mr. Powers, does this count on our grade?" a dark-haired boy in the front row asked.

Mr. Powers was a skinny, middle-aged man with thinning blond hair and horn-rimmed glasses. He wasn't the best teacher Amber had ever had, but he wasn't the worst either. He rolled his eyes at the question. "Yes, Mick, it counts against your grade. That's why it's called a quiz."

"But you didn't tell us about it," a cute blonde sitting by the door protested. "That's not fair."

"I told you the first day of class that I gave pop quizzes and that they counted," Mr. Powers explained. "This is an honors class. You should be prepared." He picked up a stack of paper and came out from behind his desk. He passed the papers down each row. "You have twenty minutes to finish," he said.

Amber took her paper from the girl in front of her. She was the last person in her row. Scanning the questions, she picked up her pen.

She finished in less than ten minutes, put her pen down and leaned back. Mr. Powers had sat back down at his desk and picked up the newspaper.

"Psst . . ."

Amber started as she realized the boy sitting across the aisle was trying to get her attention. She didn't want to be caught talking during a quiz, but when you didn't have any friends, you couldn't afford to ignore an overture from someone either. She glanced quickly to her left.

"Let me see your paper," the boy mouthed.

Amber gaped at him. She couldn't believe he was serious. Uneasily, she glanced back at the teacher. Mr. Powers now had his nose buried in the sports section.

"Come on," the kid hissed. He held out his hand. "Let me see it."

Maybe it was his tone, or maybe it was because she didn't like being ordered around, but instead of handing her paper over, she looked him straight in the eye and shook her head.

His blue eyes widened in shock. Amber had the impression he wasn't used to girls telling him "no." Well, tough, she wasn't going to risk getting caught cheating for a stranger. It wasn't like he'd gone out of his way to be nice to her.

His expression turned ugly. Real ugly. His eyes narrowed and his lips curled in a sneer. She was stunned at his reaction. For goodness sakes, it was only a quiz.

"Bitch," he mouthed.

Amber turned away. She had a funny feeling she'd just made a big mistake. Maybe she should have let him cheat off her paper. From his reaction, he didn't seem like the type to let the incident roll off him.

As the rest of the class period passed, she could sometimes feel his eyes on her. But Amber kept her attention glued to the front, refusing to let him see that he was scaring her a little.

For goodness sakes, it was only a quiz. But when the final bell rang, she got up, grabbed her backpack and started down the aisle. She stumbled, tripping over the long leg he'd just stuck out.

"Hey," she yelped.

"What's going on back there?" Mr. Powers asked. "Jack, what are you doing?" Several other students stopped and stared at them.

"Sorry about that." The kid smiled nastily at her as he got to his feet. "My foot must have slipped," he called to the teacher.

Mr. Powers looked at Amber. "Is that what happened? Are you all right?"

Amber knew he'd done it deliberately but she didn't want to make this any worse than it was. "I'm fine," she said. "It's okay."

Mr Powers nodded briefly. Without looking back, Amber hurried out of the classroom. She wasn't sure, but she thought she heard him laugh.

Her next period was lunch. Amber continued across the quad to the secluded spot next to the library. The main building of the school was two stories high and over fifty years old. Behind that was a center quad intersected with walkways and surrounded by modern buildings. Amber dumped her backpack on the raised concrete siding. She wasn't at all hungry. The ugly incident had made her lose her appetite.

She sighed. Great, just great. She'd finally made contact with someone at this school and instead of making a friend, she'd probably made an enemy.

"He tripped you deliberately," a soft voice said from behind her. "I saw him do it."

Amber whirled around. A short, slender African-American girl with wire-rimmed glasses and delicate features stared at her apprehensively.

"Yeah, I guessed as much," Amber said. "He was mad because I wouldn't let him look at my quiz paper. Is he always such a jerk?"

The girl smiled faintly. Her skin was the color of creamed coffee, her hair was pulled back in a high bun and she was dressed in a pair of jeans and a pale green knit top. She had both a backpack slung over her shoulder and an armload of books. She hunched over the books, almost as though she was trying to make herself smaller. "Pretty much. Hi, I'm Harriet Islington."

"Amber Makepeace. Who is that guy, anyway?"

"His name is Jack Redden," Harriet said. "He's one of the most popular guys on campus."

"Popular?" Amber couldn't believe it. "You've got to be kidding. Why would people like someone that obnoxious? All I did was refuse to let him cheat and he stuck his leg out so I'd trip."

"Popular probably wasn't the best word to use. I should have said he was well-known." Harriet grinned. "You can be well-known without being well-liked. Do you have lunch now?"

Puzzled by the abrupt change of subject, Amber nodded. "Yeah, I usually just sit here and read while I eat."

Harriet bit her lip. "Oh . . ." She turned as if to leave.

"But I'd love some company," Amber said quickly. "I sit and read because I don't know anyone. I'm new here. I just moved to Lansdale a few weeks ago." She watched Harriet carefully, hoping her eagerness for company wouldn't scare the other girl off. Sometimes Amber felt like she was on another planet—that she'd lost whatever social skills she'd once had and she'd never have any friends again.

But Harriet wasn't going anywhere. She smiled and set her books down next to Amber's backpack. Then she lowered her own pack, unzipped it and pulled out a brown paper bag.

Amber quickly pulled out her own lunch. "Let's sit together," she said.

They settled down on the wall. Harriet pulled a ham and cheese sandwich out of her bag. Amber had peanut butter and jelly.

"Where did you go before here?" Harriet took a bite of her sandwich.

"El Toro High School," Amber replied. She took a bite of her sandwich. "That's in Lake Forest. It's south of Los Angeles."

"I know where it is." Harriet took a box of grape juice out of her bag and stuck the little straw in the top. "My cousin goes to Dana Hills High down there. Must have been hard, moving your senior year. Did your dad change jobs or something?"

Amber hated this part. Talking about it still hurt. "My parents are dead. I moved here to live with my cousin after my mom died."

"Oh, God, I'm sorry." Harriet's face flushed with

embarrassment. "I shouldn't have said anything. I should have kept my mouth shut. . . ."

"It's a perfectly reasonable question." Amber smiled at her new friend. "That's okay, you didn't know. My mom was sick for a long time, so it wasn't like I was surprised when she passed away. But it still hurts a lot."

"Yeah, I guess it would," Harriet murmured sympathetically. "When did your mom . . ." She broke off, unable to finish the question.

"In June. Right after school got out. I stayed on in the house until it sold and then I came up here to live with my cousin. She's my legal guardian until I turn eighteen in November."

Harriet nodded and took another bite of her sandwich. "So, are you planning on going to college around here?"

"I don't know," Amber replied. "I mean, I'm going to college, but I don't have any idea where. I suppose I'll have to decide this year, won't I?"

"How'd you do on your SATs?"

"I haven't taken them yet," Amber admitted. "But my grades are good, so I don't think I'll have any problems getting in somewhere."

"My parents want me to go to San Diego."

"San Diego State?"

Harriet shook her head. "UC San Diego. They want me to study chemistry. You know how parents can be: 'Harriet's good at science so Harriet is going to study chemistry.'"

"Is that what you want to do?"

"I don't know," Harriet sighed. "I guess it'll be okay. What about you? What are you interested in?"

"Drama." Amber couldn't believe she'd actually said it out loud. But she couldn't back down now.

Harriet's eyebrows rose. "You want to be a movie star?"

"Nah, I want to study theatre," Amber said confidently. She'd never once had the nerve to voice her dream. She'd kept it buried deep inside her until those last few months before her mother died. The two of them had become totally, totally honest about everything then. It had been her mom who had forced her to really think about how she wanted to spend her life. It had been her mom who'd told her to go after her dream no matter how crazy or insecure it seemed. "There isn't any such thing as security anyway," Alicia Makepeace had said. "So you shouldn't spend a minute of this precious life doing something you don't want to do. If you want to study theatre, honey, go for it. Do it with my blessing and do it with your whole heart and soul."

"You like theatre?" Harriet asked. She tried to sound casual, but Amber could hear the excitement in her voice.

"I love it," Amber said. "I haven't been to many live performances of anything in the past couple of years, but I've managed to see *Rent* and *Phantom of the Opera*."

Harriet's face lit up. "You've seen *Rent*? Didn't you just love it? I think it's awesome . . . absolutely awesome. Who played Roger?"

"I don't know," Amber wailed. "I lost the Playbill

and didn't realize it until we'd left the theatre. But whoever he was, he was great." Discovering that Harriet shared her love of live theatre was almost a miracle to Amber. For the rest of their lunch period, they compared notes on the plays they'd seen and more important, what ones they wanted to see. When the bell rang, Amber reluctantly got to her feet and gathered up her stuff. "Are you in drama?" she asked Harriet, who was also getting her things together.

"Are you kidding?" Harriet said. "My parents wouldn't let me take it. They said it was frivolous and stupid."

"Darn, that's too bad. I have Drama Three for last period. I was hoping you were in one of the other classes."

"I wish," Harriet sighed wistfully. "I'd love to be an actress. But my parents almost had a cow when I even mentioned it."

Amber nodded sympathetically. "That's tough. Uh, do you want to eat together Monday?"

"I'd like that," Harriet replied. "Uh, look, usually I eat with my friend Mark. Do you mind if he comes along? You'll like him—he's a *Rent* fan, too."

"The more the merrier. I don't know anyone so it's nice to meet people."

Harriet laughed. "Okay, until Monday then. I'll see you."

Amber waved and then went off to her afternoon classes. By the time school was out and she was making her way to her locker, she found herself wondering if Harriet would like to do something over the weekend. But she didn't want to be pushy.

Amber darted across the quad to the other side of the life science bungalow where her locker was located. She knew it was pathetic, but she was really, really jazzed about making a new friend. She hadn't wanted to admit, even to herself, how lonely she'd been for the company of someone her own age.

She flew around the corner and then came to a dead halt. Jack Redden was standing by her locker. He cocked his head to one side and smiled. With his perfect white teeth, dark hair and blue eyes, he should have been handsome. But the mocking smirk of a grin on his broad face made him look mean and repulsive. Another boy stood next to him.

Both of them were looking at her. She hadn't realized how big Jack was. Well, she amended as she forced herself to move, maybe he wasn't a giant but he was a lot bigger than she was.

She took a deep breath and continued toward the locker. She hadn't realized how isolated this part of the campus was . . . at least there wasn't anyone around now. Redden's smile twisted into a sneer as she approached. She stopped right in front of him. Neither her nor the other kid said anything. He just stood in front of her locker, blocking her from getting into it.

She cleared her throat. "Excuse me, I need to get in there."

"Oh, is this your locker?" he asked innocently and then grinned at his buddy. "I didn't know the fresh faces on campus had been assigned lockers yet." He didn't move. But the other kid giggled. Amber glanced at him. He was a skinny boy with short red hair, deep-set brown eyes and a bunch of zits on his chin. He met

Amber's eyes for a split second before looking away. She turned her attention back to Jack Redden.

"I want to get into my locker," she said.

"You don't get it, do you?" he said, leaning into her face.

"Get what?" she asked. She stared into his eyes. Show no fear, she thought.

"That you're the new kid on the block and I'm the guy who runs things around here. This is Jack's place, understand?"

"You run things around here?" she repeated. This was unbelievable.

"Yeah, and when I tell you to give me your quiz paper, you'd damned well do it." He leaned even closer to her. She could smell the burger he'd had for lunch on his breath. She took a step backward. "This is just a warning, okay? I figure I'll cut you some slack because you're new and all. But the next time, I'm not going to be so nice."

Chapter
Two

Dear Diary,
Things could be worse, but I don't see how. I've been at this school less than a week and I've already had a run-in with the local lunatic. His name is Jack Redden and he's actually kind of good looking, but he's got a personality like Freddy Krueger. Just because I wouldn't let him cheat, he threatened me. He didn't say exactly what he'd do if I didn't hand over my paper the next time he snaps his fingers and I'm not sure I want to find out. To top it off, the creep seems to be kind of popular.

I don't know what to do. Maybe I'll talk to Celia about it. She is my guardian. If things get really bad, she'll call the school or something. No, I don't want to do that. Maybe I'll just ask the teacher to let me change seats.

What a colossal drag! It's bad enough having to

move up here and go through all these freaky changes. I shouldn't have to watch my back, too! What a way to spend my senior year.

Amber read the words she'd just written and almost cried. On paper she didn't sound near as scared as she felt. It wasn't that Jack Redden and his creepy friend had done anything to her. After he'd delivered his "warning" yesterday, the boys had walked away. Shaken, but determined not to let it show, she'd opened her locker, gotten out her books and headed for the bus stop. But she knew they'd watched her. She'd seen them out of the corner of her eye. They'd hung around at the end of the walkway glaring at her until she'd turned the corner of the building.

Amber sighed and closed her diary. Great, just great. Now what was she going to do? She didn't want to sit next to Jack Redden in class on Monday. She wouldn't sit next to him. She'd talk to the teacher. Surely Mr. Powers would let her move. She sighed again.

The next day was Saturday. The house was quiet when Amber got up. Celia and her boyfriend had taken off for Las Vegas on Friday night and weren't going to return until the wee hours of Monday morning. By late afternoon, Amber had done her laundry, cleaned the house and done all her homework.

She changed out of her cleaning clothes into a pair of shorts and a halter top, made herself a pitcher of iced tea and picked up the mystery she'd started earlier in the week. She headed for the living room and then changed her mind. She'd been inside all day, she might as well go outside. It might be hot, but it was better than sitting inside these walls.

Amber went outside and put her stuff down on the bottom step. She went to the back of the mobile home and got the TV tray. Propping it open between the two chairs, she settled in and made herself comfortable. A few minutes later, she heard the sound of her neighbor's front door opening.

"You want some company?" Mrs. Bartlett asked cheerfully. She was holding a glass of what looked like lemonade.

"Come on over," Amber called. She quickly closed her book and put it on the ground under her seat.

"How's it going?" The older woman put her drink down before slowly lowering herself into the chair. "You made any friends yet at school?"

"I've gotten to know one girl a little bit," Amber admitted. "But it's kind of hard. Most seniors already have their friends and their own groups."

She nodded. "That's what Chris told me when I mentioned you. He said moving to a new school your senior year is about the hardest thing you can do."

"That's pretty much it," Amber agreed. One part of her wanted to tell Mrs. Bartlett about her run-in with Jack Redden, but another part of her was too embarrassed. She changed the subject. "Mrs. Bartlett, do you know if the mail has come yet?"

"Oh, honey, call me Lucy. The mail comes about noon on Saturdays. Why? You waitin' for something special?"

"No, not me. My cousin is." Amber could feel her cheeks flush. She'd overheard Celia on the phone with

Dale a couple of nights ago and her cousin had been complaining that the check was late.

Celia received a check from Alicia Makepeace's estate for acting as guardian to Amber. "Maybe it'll come today," she murmured. If the envelope wasn't in today's mail, Amber decided, she'd call Mr. Lindstrom on Monday. It was bad enough being stuck here—she knew she was crimping her cousin's style. She didn't want to cost her an arm and a leg, too!

"Whew." Lucy picked up her lemonade and took a quick gulp. "It sure is hot today. How come you're not out at the pool?"

There was a really nice swimming pool as well as a Jacuzzi in the mobile home park.

"I usually wait until a little later in the day," Amber replied. "I burn easily. I always go after four o'clock."

Lucy cocked her head to one side and studied Amber thoughtfully. "With that dark brown hair of yours, it looks like you could handle the sun. But you've got such fair skin, you'd fry pretty fast. I've tried to tell Chris he ought to be careful, but he thinks I'm just a worrywart."

"My mom died of cancer," Amber said. "She made darned sure that I knew that too much sun causes skin cancer. Besides, if I'm in the sun too long, I get sick to my stomach."

"Hey, Grandma, where are you?" The male voice came from inside Lucy's mobile home.

"Out here, honey," she called.

Lucy's front door opened and a tall, muscular black-haired boy stepped out. He stopped for a split second as his gaze reached Amber, then he continued down the steps toward them.

"Hi, honey," Lucy said warmly. "I wasn't expecting to see you until tomorrow."

"My work schedule changed, so I came by today to see if you wanted me to take you to the market." He smiled at Amber as he spoke.

Amber tried not to gawk. He had a lean, intelligent face, hazel eyes and a deep tan. The faded cutoffs and green tank top fit his lean, muscled body perfectly.

"That's nice of you, dear," Lucy continued, "but I don't need anything. Janie took me yesterday. Chris, this is my neighbor, Amber Makepeace. The girl I told you about."

"Hi." He nodded to her.

"Hi," she replied. Amber was suddenly aware that the shorts and halter top she'd tossed on had seen better days.

There was a short, awkward pause, then Chris said, "I hear you just moved here a few weeks ago."

"That's right."

"You go to Lansdale High, right?"

"Right," she said. Goodness, she thought, was she so socially backward she'd forgotten how to talk to a boy? "It seems like a nice school." What else could she say? The silence returned.

"Why don't you bring out a chair and join us?" Lucy suggested. "We'd like some company."

"Thanks, Grandma," he said, his expression regretful. "But if you don't need me to take you shopping, I'm going to take off. I want to get some studying done today."

"Okay, honey. How's your mom?"

"She's fine. She's going up to the cabin tomorrow."

Lucy's eyebrows shot up in surprise. "Is your dad going?"

Chris grinned. "Nope. She's going with a friend. For once, Mom put her foot down and told him that just because he was a workaholic, that didn't mean she couldn't get out and go somewhere."

Lucy chuckled. "It'll do Sebastian good to have to look after himself for a few days. Marta spends way too much time making that man's life easy."

"Uh, look, Grandma, I've got to make tracks. I'll give you a call later this week." Chris glanced at Amber. "Nice to meet you."

"Nice to meet you, too," she muttered. God, she sounded like a twit. Why couldn't she have thought of something funny or witty?

He bent down, gave Lucy a quick kiss and then took off. Amber picked up her drink and took a long, cool sip. He really was cute. And she liked the way he was nice to his grandmother.

Maybe this place wasn't going to be so bad after all.

Celia got home so late Sunday night that Amber had already gone to bed. Amber didn't have a chance to talk to her until just before she had to catch the bus for school.

"Uh, I'm having kind of a problem in one of my classes," Amber began. She'd decided to mention the incident to Celia just in case she needed her to call the school or write a note or something.

Celia yawned and grabbed the coffeepot off the

counter. "What kind of problem?" She turned on the water.

"Well, this kid in my history class is acting like a real jerk . . ."

"Most boys that age act like jerks." She turned off the faucet and poured the water into the pot. "Did you get the mail on Saturday?" Celia asked. She dismissed Amber's problem without a second thought.

"It's on top of the TV," Amber replied. "And you don't have to worry, the check from Mr. Lindstrom arrived."

Celia turned and gave her a long, stony stare. "I wasn't worried. What made you think I was? Have you been eavesdropping on my conversations with Dale?"

"No." Amber could feel her cheeks flush red. "I just happened to hear you mention that the check was late. I'm sorry . . . Oh, darn, look at the time. I've got to rush or I'll miss my bus."

"Make sure you have your house keys," Celia called. "I won't be here this afternoon."

Amber slung her backpack onto her shoulder. "But I thought you had the afternoon off . . ." She was sure that Celia had told her she wouldn't be working and the two of them could go out. "I thought we were going to cruise the mall."

"Plans change." Celia shrugged as though the matter wasn't important. But she was unable to meet Amber's gaze. "Uh, Dale got his day off switched so the two of us are going miniature golfing. You and I can hit the mall some other time, okay?"

"Sure," Amber mumbled. But she knew there

wouldn't be another time. Celia didn't want to spend her free time with a seventeen-year-old girl. Amber decided she'd go to the mall on her own. Celia wasn't the only one who got a check from Mr. Lindstrom.

"What was it you wanted to tell me? Oh, yes, a school thing. If some stupid boy is annoying you, ignore him—that's what I always did in high school."

"It's nothing." Amber headed toward the back door. "It's not important. I can take care of it. See you later."

Celia waved and turned her attention back to the coffeepot.

Amber made it to the bus stop just in time. She hopped on board and flashed her bus pass. "How are you today?" the cheerful, middle-aged driver asked.

"Fine," she said and smiled, glad to see a friendly face. She guessed he considered her a regular now. She started for her usual seat behind him and then realized it was already taken. The bus was crowded, but she spotted a seat near the back door. Amber had to hang onto the overhead bar as she worked her way to the empty seat. A boy who looked to be her own age had the seat by the window. He glanced at her as she slid in next to him and then quickly looked away. He wore a pair of wraparound sunglasses. His mousy brown hair was parted on the side and fell across his forehead.

Amber thought she'd seen him at school. "Hi," she said as she slung her pack around and balanced it on her lap. No point in riding the two miles to school in silence.

"Hi." He didn't glance her way, just continued to look out the window.

She sighed and leaned back. Why hadn't she kept her mouth shut? What was wrong with her? She brushed her teeth and wore deodorant. Why couldn't she make contact with anyone? For goodness sakes, she wasn't a troll. Why was everyone treating her like she had lice or something? Some people even considered her pretty. Her long dark hair was shiny and healthy, her fair skin was relatively free of zits and her eyes were a really nice shade of green. She knew people didn't pick their friends on looks, but she didn't think she was repulsive. Yet she couldn't seem to get anyone except Harriet to even want to talk to her. She might as well . . .

"Uh, you go to Lansdale High, right?"

She jerked at the sound of the boy's voice. "Yeah, I'm a senior." She gave him a friendly smile, hoping he hadn't taken offense at the way she'd jumped in surprise when he'd spoken.

"Me, too." He bobbed his head and then looked back out the window.

Amber realized she'd been wrong. He wasn't stuck up, he was probably just shy. A lot of people were. "I'm Amber," she said. "Amber Makepeace."

He turned his gaze back to her. "Brandon," he murmured. "Brandon Yates."

"Do you take this bus every day?" she asked. She was fairly sure he did. She'd seen him every time she got on.

He sighed. "Yeah, I got my driver's license this summer," he explained quickly. "But I have to find a job before I can use the car. My parents won't pay for my car insurance."

"I don't know how to drive," she said. "I'm hoping to learn sometime this year." Amber put that on her list of things to mention to Mr. Lindstrom the next time they talked. She wasn't planning on living at her cousin's place forever and in California you needed to know how to drive.

"It's no big deal," Brandon said. "Any moron can steer a car."

"I'll keep that in mind if I ever get behind the wheel."

"You live around here?"

"I live at the mobile home park."

"You new at Lansdale?"

"I moved here this summer," she replied. "From Orange County. And you?"

"I've lived here all my life," he said. "Born at Lansdale Memorial, played in Lansdale Little League, go to Lansdale High, etc., etc. A real local."

Amber laughed. Brandon's dry sense of humor broke the ice. They talked easily the rest of the way to school. As they were walking across campus toward the front door, Amber spotted Jack Redden and his slimy friend pulling into the driveway leading to the student parking lot. Redden was driving a black BMW. Her laughter died as she stared at the car.

"You know Jack?" Brandon asked.

Amber shook her head. "Not really. He's in one of my classes. Is he a friend of yours?" She hoped not.

"Are you kidding?" He laughed. "I take the bus, which means I'm automatically a geek to someone like him. Uh, you like him?"

"Not much," she mumbled.

They started up the wide front steps of the main building. "A lot of girls have crushes on him," Brandon continued. "The fact that Redden's got the social skills of a slug and the IQ of an ostrich doesn't seem to keep him from getting dates."

"There's no accounting for taste." Amber laughed and pulled open the front door. Just inside, she stopped and pointed over his shoulder toward the far end of the hall. "My first class is Spanish Four. It's down that way."

"Mine's advanced biology, over in the science building." He whipped off his glasses. She saw that his eyes were a deep, dark brown. "Uh, what bus do you take home?" he asked.

"The two thirty-eight," she said. "My last class is sixth period. I took extra units my sophomore and junior years."

"Well, uh, maybe I'll see you on the bus." He nodded to her and started down the hall toward the door leading to the quad.

"See you," she called. Amber hurried to her first period class. It felt good to finally start meeting people. Despite her run-in with Jack Redden and his creepy friend, maybe Lansdale High wouldn't be such an ordeal after all. Friday she'd met Harriet and this morning she'd met Brandon. If she kept this up, by the time Thanksgiving rolled around she'd be the most popular girl on campus. Amber laughed to herself as she darted into the class and took her seat.

She was in good spirits for the rest of the morning. By the time the bell rang for the passing period before her history class, she'd decided to ask to have her seat changed. She flew down the hall, determined to get there early so she could talk to the teacher privately.

Mr. Powers was sitting at his desk, his nose in the *Los Angeles Times* when she walked into the room. He didn't look up.

Amber stood beside his desk and cleared her throat. "Mr. Powers, sir. Can I speak with you a moment?"

"Certainly," He peered at her over the top of the sports section. "And you are . . ."

"I'm Amber Makepeace," she said. "I'm in your class. I sit back there." She pointed toward the back of the room. "That's what I want to talk to you about. I want to change seats."

"Change seats?" He frowned.

That wasn't a good sign.

"That might be difficult." Mr. Powers put the paper down and stared out at the classroom. "This class is full. There aren't any extra spaces. Why do you want to move?"

Amber debated for a split second. "I can't see from the back. I think it's my eyesight. Actually, I'm going to get my eyes checked soon."

She wasn't sure why she didn't tell the teacher the truth. Maybe it was because during her mother's illness she'd learned that in dealing with doctors, hospitals, insurance companies, school administrators and even Mr. Lindstrom the best way to get what you needed was to keep your explanation as simple as possible. She figured the same logic was true of teachers. Mr. Powers would be much more likely to help her if he thought it was a physical problem with her eyes rather than a potential problem with the school bully.

Teachers hated dealing with stuff like that. Especially as Redden hadn't really done anything to her.

"Well, if you can't see . . ." Mr. Powers shook his head. "I suppose we can ask if someone will change places with you."

Other kids were drifting into the room. Amber couldn't believe it. He was going to ask someone to switch with her? Voluntarily? She had a sinking feeling in her stomach. When she'd come into the classroom on the first day, the only empty seats there'd been in the room had been around Jack Redden. Maybe there'd been a reason for that.

"Go ahead and sit down," he instructed, "and as soon as class starts, we'll see what we can do." He turned his attention back to the newspaper spread on his desk.

Amber walked to her seat. She opened her backpack and took out her book. She didn't open it until she spotted Jack coming through the door. She avoided looking his way as she heard him swing into his seat. The class filled up quickly and the bell rang. Amber held her breath as Mr. Powers got up. "Before we start today, is there anyone here in the front who'll trade seats with uh . . ." He looked at her. "What did you say your name was?"

"Amber," she said. The whole class was staring at her.

"Amber, back there." He pointed to her. "She can't see very well. Who'll volunteer and do their good deed for the day?" He looked around. The clock ticked off ten long seconds.

No hands went up.

Amber couldn't believe it.

"Come on, now," Mr. Powers said. "Surely one of you has twenty-twenty vision."

Amber gazed quickly around the room. As soon as her eyes met someone's, they'd look away. She suddenly understood exactly what was going on. Her instincts had been right. No one in their right mind wanted to sit next to Jack Redden.

"I'll trade with her."

"That's not going to do her a lot of good, Jack," the teacher pointed out. "You sit right next to her. But thanks anyway."

Amber cringed. She glanced in Redden's direction. He gave her a taunting smirk of a smile. She looked away. She had the feeling something really bad had just happened.

She'd blown this. Big-time. Now Jack knew she'd asked to have her seat changed, knew she was trying to get away from him. Moreover, everyone in class knew it, too. She could see it in their faces. So could Jack. She had a feeling he wouldn't forgive her for that. If the teacher had quietly moved her without making a big deal of it, there was an outside chance Jack wouldn't have thought anything of it. People were always moving around at the beginning of the semester.

"Sorry, Amber." Mr. Powers shook his head in disgust. "It looks like your classmates are too selfish to help out. You'll have to wait until someone leaves or changes classes. All right, class, take out your books and open them to chapter two."

Amber swallowed hard and opened her book. She

kept her attention front and center for the remainder of the class period. But she could feel Redden's eyes on her. It wasn't a nice feeling either.

When the bell rang, she was ready. Her backpack was unzipped and all her papers were in her notebook. She slapped the book in the pack and got out of her seat. She swung around behind her desk and went up the aisle between the seats and the wall. Most of the kids were still putting their stuff together when she hit the door and escaped.

Amber hated acting like such a coward, but she wanted to get as far away from Redden as she could. She had a bad feeling about him. Mr. Powers hadn't been any help, so Amber decided that if Jack Redden kept on giving her grief, she'd go to the principal. She didn't like being a snitch, but she wasn't going to spend her senior year being scared out of her wits either.

When she reached her spot by the library, she sank down on the concrete siding. Her heart pounded and sweat trickled down her back. Closing her eyes, she told herself to lighten up. She was making too much of it. It was only one class after all.

"Hey, you asleep or what?"

Amber jerked and turned to see Harriet approaching. A tall skinny kid with glasses and short blond hair was with her. "Hi," she said.

"This is Mark Hayes." Harriet introduced her companion. "He's the guy I was telling you about."

"The *Rent*head." Amber grinned. "Hi, Mark."

"Hi." He returned her smile. "And yeah, I'm a

*Rent*head. I've seen it three times: in L.A., San Francisco and in New York on Broadway."

"Three times! That's not fair, I only got to see it once," Amber exclaimed with a laugh. She scooted over so Harriet could sit down next to her. "I saw it when it came to Orange County. It was great. I'm dying to see it again."

"Me, too. Believe it or not, three isn't very many," he said. He slung his backpack onto the top of the wall and unzipped it. Sticking his hand inside, he pulled out a crumpled brown lunch bag. "I know people who have seen it ten or twenty times. There's one guy in New York who's seen it over three hundred times."

"Really?" Amber pulled her own lunch bag out of her pack.

"He doesn't really know these people," Harriet interjected. "He's met them on-line. There're a lot of chat rooms and sites devoted to the show."

"You mean on the Internet?" Amber asked. She was genuinely curious. She'd never had a chance to surf the 'Net. She had her own computer, but it was an older model without a modem.

"I know them," Mark protested. "Just because you haven't met someone face-to-face doesn't mean you don't know them. And I have met some of them in person.

"Besides, you're one to talk. What about those *Phantom of the Opera* freaks you're always talking to?"

"They're not freaks," Harriet yelped, "they're my friends . . . Oh, okay, I get your point. But still, I'm not as bad as you are. I don't spend every waking moment on the 'Net."

"It's not like there's much else to do around here," he said. He took out a sandwich and tossed the bag on top of the concrete wall next to his pack.

"Aren't there football games and stuff like that?" Amber asked.

Harriet and Mark exchanged a quick look. Then Harriet said, "Sure, if you're into all that sports kind of stuff. Are you?"

"I don't know," Amber explained. "I've never been to one."

"Did you go to a girls' school or something?" Mark asked.

"No, I went to a regular high school." Amber looked away. "But, uh, for the past few years I was taking care of my mom. I never got to do anything at school. Don't get me wrong, I'm not upset about missing anything. I just always thought I'd go to one if I got the chance, that's all."

"There's one this Friday night," Harriet said. "Why don't we all go? It's the first game of the season."

"Since when did you become a football fan?" Mark asked her. But he was smiling.

"Since I decided it would be stupid if I didn't go to at least one game before I graduate." She looked at Amber. "You want to go?"

"I'd love to," Amber replied eagerly. "Uh, I don't know how to drive. How are we going to get there?"

"It's a home game," Mark said. He rolled the empty sandwich bag into a ball and shot it into the trash container a few feet away. "I can drive. Then we can go and get a burger or something afterward. That okay with you two?"

"Yup." Harriet pulled an apple out of her pack and looked at Amber. "Where do you live?"

"Do you know the mobile home park up at the end of Twin Oaks Boulevard?" she asked. "I live there. But I'll give you my phone number—that way I can meet you outside. The place is huge and it'll be hard for you to find the unit unless I draw you a map."

"Do you live with your dad?" Mark asked softly. Apparently Harriet had tipped him off that her mom was dead.

Amber shook her head. "I live with my cousin. She's my guardian."

They chatted like old friends as they finished their lunch. When the bell rang, Amber was so relaxed she'd almost forgotten that she was still stuck sitting next to Jack the Jerk, as she now thought of him.

The day got warmer as the afternoon wore on. By the time the last class was over and she was heading down the walkway to her locker, she was hot and tired. She hoped the air-conditioning on the bus was working today. Friday it had been broken and they'd driven all the way across town with hot air blowing in their faces.

She noticed that a couple of kids were staring at her as she walked. She brushed her hand over her face, thinking she might have gotten an ink smudge on her nose or something. Then she reached her locker and her mouth dropped open in shock. She couldn't believe this.

The word *bitch* was scrawled across the locker in large, crude, red block letters.

She felt like she'd been punched in the stomach.

She was so stunned it took her a moment to react. She reached up and touched the "h". It hadn't had time to dry, so it smeared easily.

Amber quickly unzipped her pack, stuck her hand inside and grabbed at the folded tissue she'd tossed in when her nose was running last week. She reached up and swiped at the offending word, smearing it across the metal so that it was unrecognizable. She shook her head in disgust. Now it just looked like someone had slapped red paint on the locker.

She looked down at the stained tissue in her hand and then looked around. Luckily she got out of class earlier than most of the kids, so except for a boy at the far end of the walkway, no one was around. Amber opened her locker and pulled out her books. She slammed it shut. She'd have to report this to the office, but she didn't want to do it now. She was too depressed. What a mean, lousy thing to do!

She trudged up the walkway, rounded the corner and then came to a dead stop.

Jack Redden and his friend were standing there, waiting for her.

She backed up a few steps.

Redden gave her an ugly smile. "Hey, what's wrong? You look upset about something."

"I am upset," she said. "That was an awful thing to do."

"Was it? Was it really? Let me tell you something, girlie. You ain't seen nothing yet."

Chapter
Three

Dear Diary,
This is getting scary. Jack Redden is crazy. Absolutely
crazy. I don't know why the local bully is singling me out,
but I'm not going to put up with it. I know that Celia
doesn't know much about teenagers and all that, but—
jeez—she's got to do something. I'm going to talk to her
tomorrow, tell her to call the school and get them to
make this creep leave me alone . . .

She looked up as the phone rang. Tossing her diary
to one side, she grabbed the receiver, hoping it was
Celia. She usually called when she was going to be
home late.

"Hello," she said.

"Uh, hi, it's Harriet. You know, from school. I hope
you don't mind my calling."

Amber was surprised at the question. Didn't Harriet talk to her other friends? "No, of course not. I wouldn't have given you my number if I hadn't wanted you to call. What's up? You forget what our homework assignment is tonight?"

"I wish I could." Harriet laughed. "I just called to say I was sorry I didn't volunteer to change places with you today in History."

"Why should you want to sit next to Jack the Creep?" Amber sighed. "I was hoping a guy would offer to change seats with me. You know, someone twice Redden's size who he wouldn't mess with."

"No such luck," Harriet said. "No one wants to sit near him. The only reason he has any friends at all is because he has the cash to buy their loyalty. His folks are really loaded and they keep Jacky boy well suppled in twenties. Other people he bullies."

"You mean I'm not the first person he's pushed around?" Amber asked. She picked up the cordless phone and wandered out into the living room.

"Not by a long shot," Harriet said disgustedly. "Our freshman year he tortured Jake Grant and sophomore year it was Tom Halloway. Last year it was Eric Tran. It got so bad Eric's parents pulled him out and sent him to his uncle's to live so he could go to school in Oxnard."

Amber's stomach heaved. She didn't like hearing this. Didn't like it at all. "So I'm the first girl he's bullied?"

"That's what it looks like," Harriet said sympathetically. "But you know, he might just be fooling around, trying to get your attention or something. You know, like he's got a crush on you."

"Now that's even scarier." Amber propped her feet up on the coffee table. One of the few nice things about living with Celia was that she didn't care about scratching the furniture and stuff like that. "Why doesn't someone do something about him?"

"Like what?" Harriet asked. "Redden's not stupid. He never actually hurts anyone and he makes sure that the harassment is just this side of the line. You know, like he did today when he volunteered to trade seats with you while at the same time giving you one of those looks that says the complete opposite. You know what I mean?"

"He's slick all right." She told Harriet about her locker and his threats.

"What a creep!" Harriet exclaimed. "That is so like Jack. Trust him to pick on the new kid in town. But that's always been the way he operates. His victims are always the ones who can't really fight back."

"What do you mean?"

"I mean he always lays into someone who is disadvantaged in some way. Jake Grant, that kid he bullied in his freshman year, he didn't have a father and his mom was in a mental institution. Poor Jake lived with his grandmother in a tiny apartment on Twin Oaks Boulevard. Tom Halloway—he was borderline mentally retarded. He didn't stand a chance against Redden. Eric Tran's family is dirt poor . . ." She broke off as she realized what she was saying. "Oh, God, I'm sorry. I didn't mean to imply . . ."

"It's okay," Amber said quickly. "I know what you meant. I'm new in town and I'm an orphan." Amber didn't like to think of herself as disadvantaged. "And I guess that living in a mobile home park doesn't help either."

"I didn't mean anything," Harriet stuttered. "There's nothing wrong with mobile homes . . ."

"Stop apologizing," Amber insisted. "I understand what you were saying." She didn't bother to tell Harriet that she was far from poor. "And I guess I'm going to have to go to the principal and raise a fuss. Do you think that'll work? That he'll leave me alone?"

"He might," Harriet replied, but she sounded doubtful. "I mean, the others were all guys. This is different. If the school doesn't do something, you can sue them for sexual harassment or something."

Amber closed her eyes briefly. "This isn't the way I wanted to spend my senior year."

"I'm sorry," Harriet said softly. "It must be awful for you. New to the school and then all this sick stuff from Jack!"

"I'm not going to let that bastard ruin my senior year," Amber vowed.

"Good. Let's talk about Friday night instead." Harriet sounded relieved to change the subject. "What are you going to wear? It'll still be pretty warm."

Amber eagerly got into the spirit of making plans for Friday night. She'd never had the chance to hang out with her friends before and she was determined to make the most of it. They chatted for a good hour and then Harriet said, "Oh, damn, my parents just pulled in the driveway. I've got to go."

"Okay, I'll see you tomorrow."

"Cool. Gotta run." The phone went dead in Amber's hand. Puzzled, she stared at it for a moment and then shrugged. Maybe Harriet's parents didn't like her talking on the phone? Whatever. When she and Harriet became better friends, she'd find out.

Amber glanced at the clock. It was almost six. Celia had come home early this morning, taken a quick shower and then gone to work. She ought to be home soon. By half past at least.

But when she wasn't home by seven, Amber knew her cousin had probably gone out with her boyfriend. She ate a carton of cherry yogurt for dinner, finished her homework, took a shower and then turned on the TV. She was determined to talk to Celia, even if she had to sit up half the night.

At ten-thirty, the front door opened and Celia stepped inside. The heat had taken its toll on her. Her white cotton short-sleeved blouse was damp with sweat, her short yellow skirt was wrinkled and there were dark smudges under her eyes where her mascara had run. "You still up?" she asked in surprise when she spotted Amber on the couch. "Something good on TV?"

"I have to talk to you," Amber said. "It's important."

Celia sighed. "Can't it wait until morning? I'm beat." She tossed her purse on the couch and kicked off her high-heeled sandals. "I'm really tired."

Amber hesitated. She knew she was a burden to her cousin. She did her best not to clutter up Celia's life with any more hassles than necessary. Maybe she could handle this on her own? Maybe she could talk to the principal herself. She made up her mind. "Yeah, you look it. It's okay." She got to her feet and headed for her bedroom. "It's not that important."

"You sure?" Celia said around a wide yawn. "You know, I'm always here for you. You can always come to me, you know."

"It's not important," Amber called over her shoulder.

"Okay, I'll see you in the morning. Good night, Amber."

Amber went into her bedroom, flopped down on the bed and stared at the ceiling. She didn't know what to do. Every time she tried to talk to Celia she ended up backing down because her cousin made her feel so guilty. But what if the principal wouldn't listen? What if he didn't believe her?

"He has to believe me," she said to herself as she rolled onto her stomach. "From what Harriet said, the whole school knows that Redden's a bully."

Deciding to talk to the principal and actually getting in to see the man were two different things, Amber discovered the next morning when she went into the administration office. The room was bisected by a long counter. On her side, there were a dozen students lined up to get their readmits. On the other side were the secretary's desk and two private offices—the principal's and the vice principal's.

"Mr. Dankers is very busy," the tall, sour-looking secretary informed her. "You can't just come waltzing in here and demand to see him."

"I didn't do that," Amber protested quietly. "I asked to see him."

"Well, you can't." She turned and went back to her desk.

"Hey, Mrs. Larchmont, give her a break. It's not like anyone else wants to see old Dankers. He's not that big a draw."

"Mind your own business Garth, or you'll be right back in detention." The woman snapped at a short, pudgy kid wearing baggy jeans and a torn gray sweat-shirt. His hair was blue and spiked straight up. He grinned at Amber.

Amber grinned back, but then quickly changed her expression when she saw Mrs. Larchmont's ferocious glare. "Get to your classroom," the woman snapped. Amber wasn't sure if she was talking to her or to Garth so she said, "I'll go as soon as I've seen the principal."

The woman's eyes narrowed. "Why do you want to see him?"

Amber wasn't about to say the real reason. There were half a dozen kids in that readmit line and all of them were obviously listening to her battle of wills with the dragon lady. She already had enough trouble with Jack Redden. She didn't want him finding out she'd snitched on him before she even got a chance to say anything. "It's personal," she replied.

"I see. Well, I'll have to check his calendar. Come back this afternoon and I'll see when he has time available."

"Can't you check now?" Amber asked. She kept her tone polite, but she wasn't about to leave without at least an appointment. "According to all the school lit-erature my guardian received from the board of educa-tion, this district has an open-door policy. A policy that specifically states that students have the right to take concerns and problems to the appropriate administrator."

From the readmit line several kids laughed. Mrs. Larchmont's face flushed with anger, but the mention of the board of education did the trick. Amber was glad she'd taken the time to read the district's brochure this morning when she'd gotten up.

"Wait a minute, then," the woman said grudgingly. "I'll see when he's available."

She disappeared into the office. She was gone a good five minutes. Amber heard the first bell ring and knew she'd be tardy for class, but she wasn't going to leave. Not without an appointment.

A moment later Mrs. Larchmont returned. "It'll be at least two weeks before Mr. Dankers can see you," she said with a smug smile. "He's fully booked with other, more urgent matters."

Amber bit her lip. What was she going to do? "Maybe I can help," a man's voice said from behind her.

Amber whirled around and found herself staring at a dark-haired man with horn-rimmed glasses. She'd seen him on campus before.

"This girl wants to talk to Mr. Dankers," Mrs. Larchmont said quickly. "She doesn't seem to understand that she can't just come in here and demand to see the principal."

"I didn't do that," Amber said earnestly. "I simply wanted to make an appointment to see him. An appointment I'm legally entitled to have. I've got a problem and I need some help dealing with it. I don't know why Mrs. Larchmont is trying to make it seem like I stomped in here like some spoiled princess demanding an audience. What am I supposed to do to get a little help here, slit my wrists?" Embarrassed by her outburst, Amber clamped her mouth shut.

"You don't have to slit your wrists," the man said quickly. He cut a fast, hard glare at the secretary who was now turning beet red with anger. "I'm Jim Mullins, the vice principal. Come on into my office and let's see how I can help." He ushered Amber behind the counter and into his office.

"Have a seat," he invited as he dumped his briefcase on the floor next to an overflowing bookcase. Amber sat down on one of the two hard-backed chairs opposite the messy desk. On the wall there was a giant poster advertising the drama club's presentation of *Our Town*. Next to that was a huge roster of the upcoming football games.

Mr. Mullins slid into the chair behind the desk. He pushed his glasses up his nose and smiled at Amber. "Okay, what's the problem here—and no suicide threats, please! We take them seriously here."

Amber wasn't sure where to begin. For days now she'd been trying so hard to get someone to listen to her that now that she actually had someone's ear, she wasn't certain exactly what she should say. "I'm being bullied," she blurted out.

Mr. Mullins's concerned expression disappeared. He stared at her blankly. "Bullied?" He repeated the word slowly like he'd never heard it before. Amber didn't think that was a good sign. "You want to be a bit more specific?"

She took a deep breath. "I'm new to this school. This is my senior year. The bullying started the first week of school. This boy named Jack Redden got really ticked off when I wouldn't show him my quiz paper. He's had it in for me ever since."

He nodded encouragingly. "Go on."

Amber told him everything. By the time she was finished, she was struggling not to cry.

Mr. Mullins looked away and gave her a moment to pull herself together before he started speaking. "Did you tell your teacher the reason you wanted to change seats?" he asked softly.

"No, I couldn't," she replied. "I was afraid it would make things worse if Redden thought I'd snitched on him. But that was dumb. When Mr. Powers asked for a volunteer to switch with me, Redden figured it out."

"I see." Mr. Mullins leaned forward and picked up a pen. He jotted down a few notes and then he looked back at Amber and smiled. "Don't worry, I'll make sure you don't have to sit next to this boy anymore. And let me know if he bothers you again. I want you to enjoy your senior year here at Lansdale."

Amber was confused. "Bothers me again?" she repeated. "You are going to do something about him now, aren't you?"

"Do what?" Mr. Mullins asked. "Other than have you change seats, there isn't much we can do. Has he directly threatened you?"

"Yes. I told you what he said."

Mr. Mullins nodded sympathetically. "Did he say it in front of anyone? Any witnesses?"

"His friend was there. He's a skinny kid with red hair and tons of zits."

Mr. Mullins held up his hand. "I know who you're talking about. That's Billy Palato."

"Can't you call him in here? Get him to tell you the truth. Tell you that Jack threatened me?"

"Hold on! We're not the gestapo here," Mr. Mullins replied. "I'll have a word with him and see what he has to say. That's all I can promise you at this point. If he confirms what you say happened, then I'll take this matter further."

Amber knew what that meant. The kid wouldn't say one word against his friend. "That means you can't do anything now—it's my word against Jack's?"

"More or less," Mr. Mullins admitted. "I can't discipline him without either someone else verifying your story about being threatened or some other act of bullying. But don't worry, I'll have a word with Jack. Tell him to leave you alone. That's really all we can do."

"But you will talk to him?" Amber asked quickly.

"Of course I will," Mr. Mullins assured her. He smiled. "I'm sure it'll be fine. Don't worry. He's probably not meaning to scare you so much. He's probably just being a little boisterous and doesn't realize how seriously you're taking things."

Her heart sank. They thought she was the one taking things too seriously. "You've got to be kidding. What about all the other kids he's bullied?"

Mr. Mullins's smile faltered. He got to his feet. "I'm not sure what you're talking about, but don't be concerned. I'll talk to Jack. I'm sure he's just being a bit high-spirited." He picked up a small pad of paper and scribbled on it. Ripping the top sheet off, he handed it to Amber. "Here, this is your readmit into your first period class. Don't worry about a thing. I'll make sure you change seats in your history class. Run along now, you don't want to be too late."

Amber had no choice. She reached over and took the slip of paper. "Thank you for seeing me," she said as she went to the door. She was very confused. What was going on here?

"Let me know how things are going, Amber," Mr. Mullins called after her. "And my door is always open to students with emotional problems."

She froze for a split second and then turned back to him. "I don't think complaining about being bullied means I have emotional problems," she said, looking the vice principal straight in the eye. "I think it means that someone around here isn't doing a very good job defending students' rights."

His smile vanished completely.

Amber yanked open the door and left. She had the feeling the entire interview had been a complete waste of time.

But she was wrong.

Mr. Powers called her over to his desk as soon as she walked into her history class. He put his paper down and frowned at her. "You should have told me you were having problems with Redden," he said accusingly. "I'd have made sure you changed seats if I'd known that was the problem. I didn't like hearing about it from the vice principal."

Amber shrugged. She didn't trust herself to speak. She was afraid she'd start crying. She wasn't sure why she was letting this get to her, but she couldn't help herself.

Since seeing the vice principal, she'd felt worse and worse. Depressed. Miserable. She felt like she was completely alone on the planet and that no one gave a hoot about her or how scared she was. "I guess I should have said something," she muttered. "I'm sorry."

"That's okay." He sighed. "I know it can be hard to speak up, especially when you're new. I should have guessed what was going on. Jack's got quite a reputation. Anyway, let's find you a new seat." He looked at the room and then pointed to the first desk in the row nearest the door. "Sit there. That's John Berry's seat. He's a very popular kid and he's on the varsity football team. I don't think Redden has enough nerve to try anything on him."

"Thanks, Mr. Powers," Amber said gratefully. She sat down as the other kids began pouring into the room. She popped her backpack under the chair and took out her notebook. Flipping open the notebook, Amber watched the door out of the corner of her eye. Redden usually came in the back door, but she wanted to be on the alert just in case. But it wasn't Jack Redden who stopped by her desk, it was a tall, good-looking boy with dark hair. "Uh, I think you're in my seat," he said quietly.

"John, can you step outside with me for a moment," Mr. Powers said before Amber could speak. "I'd like to have a word with you."

"Sure," John said good-naturedly. A few minutes later, he and the teacher came back inside. John nodded and smiled at Amber as he made his way to the back of the class. Amber sighed in relief. Thank goodness, she thought. At least she didn't have to sit next to the creep anymore. Maybe things weren't as bad as she'd thought.

A tall, very pretty blonde slipped into the seat next to Amber's. She frowned. "What are you doing there? That's John's seat."

"We changed places." She gave her a friendly smile. "I'm Amber Makepeace. What's your name?"

"Julie Steadman," she muttered. She looked at the back of the class for a moment and then glared at Amber before she turned her attention to the teacher.

Amber's spirits sunk. Julie Steadman wasn't a happy camper. She was obviously ticked because John had moved. Great, Amber thought, just great. That's all she needed—to make even more enemies. She sighed silently and fought off another wave of depression. For every step forward she took, someone shoved her back three. But then she decided that was stupid. Why should she care what some dumb blonde thought of her? It wasn't like they'd have been friends anyway.

As soon as the bell rang, Amber made her escape. She'd almost made it around the side of the building when someone grabbed her arm. Whirling around, she jerked her elbow free. "Oh, it's you." She almost laughed in relief. "I'm sorry. I thought it was the Creep."

"The creep?" Harriet giggled. "I take it you mean Jack. Don't worry, he took off the other way, toward the student parking lot. He probably wants to slash some tires. Come on, let's go eat. Mark's waiting for us."

The two girls fell into step together and hurried across the quad. Mark was already there, munching on a peanut butter sandwich. "Hi. How's it goin'?"

Amber flung her backpack on the top of the wall next to Mark's. "A little better than it was," she said as she unzipped the top and pulled out the lunch bag.

"At least she isn't sitting next to the Creep anymore," Harriet chimed in. "Mr. Powers finally let her move."

"Only after I went and complained to the vice principal." Amber opened her bag and pulled out a ham sandwich.

"You went and saw Mr. Mullins?" Mark asked around a mouthful of sandwich.

"Yeah, but I don't know if it's going to do any good," Amber muttered. "I don't want to be negative about it, but I kinda got the impression he thought I was the one with the problem. Not Jack."

"That's always the way he sees it." Mark snorted in disgust. "Redden's parents donated fifty thousand bucks to the athletic department his freshman year. Ever since then, he's gotten away with murder. Mullins is the worst, though. He acts like he really cares and like he's going to do something about it, like he's going to take care of it and then he doesn't do diddly because he's scared of Redden's old man."

"How do you know so much about it?" Harriet asked. She pushed her glasses up her nose and stared at Mark curiously.

Mark shrugged. "One of his victims was a good friend of mine."

"Who?" Harriet asked. "The kid that Redden bullied last year? The one that got pulled out of school?"

"Not him." Mark shook his head. "Jake Grant. You remember him, he left in our freshman year. He was my best friend."

"I didn't know you two were buds."

"We were. I know what Jake went through. His grandmother complained and everything, but the school didn't do anything. She ended up pulling him out of school after he overdosed on some pain pills. The school's attitude was that the suicide attempt just showed what an unstable kid he was all along. If it'd been me, I'd have sued the crap out of 'em. But Jake's grandma didn't have the money for a lawyer. She ended up moving so Jake could go to school in Ventura."

"That's so sick," Harriet said. "It's so unfair. When are they going to do something? When Jack actually kills someone?"

"Gee, thanks," Amber muttered.

"Oh, no, I didn't mean that," Harriet said quickly. She look stricken. "Jack's a bully and a jerk, but he's not a complete moron. Even his folks couldn't bail him out if he got violent. Especially with a girl."

Amber wasn't so sure. But she hoped that Harriet was right.

By the time school ended and she was heading for the bus stop, she felt a little better. Some of her depression had eased. She hadn't seen Redden since history. He hadn't shown up at her locker. Neither had his friend. Amber had decided if she saw either of them again, she was going to tell them to their faces what she thought of them—that they were a pair of slimy, despicable cowards.

She just made the bus. She hopped on, flashed her bus pass at the driver and started down the aisle. The bus was crowded and Brandon Yates was sitting at the back. He gave a shy wave.

Hanging onto the top rail, she made her way to the back. "Hi," she said as she sat down next to him.

"Hi, how're you doing?"

"Fine. What's up, anything interesting?"

Brandon pulled his sunglasses off. "Only if you call two hours of calculus homework interesting. I call it criminal, but that doesn't stop teachers from assigning it."

"Yeah, I've got a lot of homework, too," Amber replied. She really didn't; most of her classes were fairly easy. That was one of the few good things to come out of her mother's illness. She'd taken extra credits and all her hard classes because she was always at home and always had plenty of time to study.

They chatted for the rest of the trip across town. As they neared her stop, she began gathering her things. "I'm beat. I think I'll go for a swim when I get home."

"That sounds cool. I wish we had a pool," Brandon said. "Uh, could you give me your phone number? Sometimes my friend Andrew picks me up for school. We could give you a lift, too—if I had your number."

"That'd be great," Amber replied. She'd always fantasized about going to school in a car full of kids. It was silly, but she didn't care.

He thrust a paper and pen at her. "Write it down; I've got a terrible memory."

She scribbled it on the paper and handed it back to him "A ride to school would be great." She grabbed her pack and got up just as they reached her stop. "See you tomorrow."

She hopped off the bus and waited for it to pull away. The stop was in front of the mobile home park, but it was at the far end away from the entrance. And the place was huge. Amber hoisted her pack comfortably and started across the street. Just as she reached the middle of the busy road, a car came roaring around the bend. She had enough time to clear the intersection, but she had to make a run for it. "Hey," she called as she stumbled onto the grass. "Hasn't anyone ever told you the pedestrian has the right-of-way?"

But the car had sped up the street. Amber shook her head in disgust and took a deep breath. Her heart raced and her throat was dry. Jeez, she thought, for such a quiet place it sure was dangerous. You took your life in your hands just by crossing the street. Lansdale is scarier than you would think.

Again, she glared up the road. Jerk. The whole thing had happened so fast she hadn't really gotten a good look at the driver. But as she stared at the pale gray asphalt, something niggled at the back of her mind. It was a man driving, she was sure, and the car had been a black BMW. She was no expert, but she could recognize some models. Amber went utterly still as she realized where she'd seen the car before.

It had been earlier this week, when she and Brandon Yates were walking up the school steps. She'd seen it come around the corner, headed for the student parking lot.

It was Jack's car.

Amber's stomach knotted in fear. What on earth was she going to do? This guy was a maniac. She shook her head and then hurried toward the entrance to the park.

She'd call the police, that's what she'd do. She'd call the police and tell them this boy was trying to hurt her. That he'd tried to run her down with his BMW.

Her fingers shook as she pulled out her house keys and unlocked the front door. She got it open and flew inside. Dumping her backpack on the floor, Amber raced for the telephone. She was reaching for it when it suddenly rang.

Her heart flew into her throat. "Hello?"

"Amber, it's me, Harriet."

"Oh Harriet, thank God it's you."

"What's wrong? Are you okay?" Harriet asked anxiously.

"I just had the most awful experience. When I got off the bus, Jack Redden almost ran me down with his car."

"Are you sure?"

"Of course I'm sure," Amber cried. "It was deliberate. He came right at me."

"Oh my God," Harriet gasped. "What a bastard. What a colossal bastard. Are you okay? Did you get hurt?"

"I'm fine. He actually didn't come that close to hitting me, but I did have to make a leap for it. I was just getting ready to call the police."

"Did anyone see it happen?" Harriet asked softly.

Amber sighed. "No. I don't think so. Or if someone did they sure kept quiet about it. I mean, no one came out and there weren't any cars on the street."

"You know what he'll say, don't you?"

"Yeah, he'll claim he was nowhere near here and that slimy friend of his will back him up."

"That's right. Once again it'll be your word against his. But don't worry, one of these days Jack Redden will be too clever for his own good. One of these days, he'll blow it in front of witnesses."

Chapter
Four

Dear Diary,
Now I'm really ticked. It was one thing to harass me at school, but he's gone too far. If I hadn't leapt for the curb, I'd be splattered all over the road. I'm not going to wait for him to "blow it in front of witnesses" either. I don't care whether Celia likes it or not, she's got to get involved. She's got to do something.

I don't care how late I have to stay up tonight, I'm going to make her understand she's got to help me. I know that Mr. Mullins didn't take me seriously today. He thinks I'm the one with the problem.

Amber glanced at the clock on the top of the TV. It was almost eleven. Yawning, she closed her diary, got up and went to her bedroom. The bed looked so inviting and she was so tired, but darn it, she was going to talk to her cousin if it meant sitting up all night.

She put the diary in her bedside table and then went into the kitchen. She might as well grab a Coke, maybe the caffeine would help her stay awake. Opening the fridge, she grabbed a can of soda, popped the top and took a long swig. She went over to the kitchen table and sat down. She and Celia had shared a meal at this table exactly once, the first night she'd come here. Since then, they'd either eaten in front of the TV or they'd eaten on their own. Usually Amber ate on her own.

Tears filled her eyes. She blinked hard to fight them back. God, she was so lonely. She missed her mom so much. She was stuck at a new school with no real friends and she was living with a woman who totally ignored her. What was she supposed to do? It wasn't just Jack Redden and his bullying that was bothering her, it was everything. But mainly, it was the loneliness. It was feeling like she had no one to turn to, no one to help her. For over two years she'd taken care of her mom and now she'd give anything, absolutely anything, to have her mother back.

Even for just a few minutes.

Her mom would know what to do. Her mom would rip Jack Redden's throat out if she had to, to protect her baby.

But there was no one to protect her now.

Except her cousin. Darn it, Amber swiped the tears from her eyes. She'd done her best not to interfere in Celia's life, but for crying out loud, the woman was getting paid to take care of her.

Amber got up, went to the bathroom and washed her face. She didn't want to be a blubbering idiot when she talked to Celia. When she came out, her cousin was sitting on the couch.

"Hi," Celia said brightly. "How ya doing? Sorry I was so late getting home, but Dale and I went out to celebrate. It was his birthday."

"That's nice," Amber muttered. "Uh, look, Celia, I've got . . ."

"You've got a birthday coming up soon," her cousin interrupted. "Bet you're excited about that. You'll be eighteen. That's one of the biggies. Sure was for me."

"Yeah, I guess so. Uh, look, Celia, I really need some help here."

"Help? For what?"

"There's a guy at school who's been harassing me," Amber blurted out. "And the school doesn't seem to care."

"Harassin' you how?"

Amber blinked at the way Celia's words slurred. She cocked her head to one side and studied her cousin closely. Celia's face was flushed, her eyes were unusually bright and she was grinning from ear to ear.

Amber was no expert, but she was fairly sure Celia was drunk. "Uh, are you all right?"

"'Course I'm all right." Celia belched. "Oops, sorry." She giggled and plopped back against the couch cushions. "This is comfy. Uhm . . . maybe I'll sleep here tonight."

Amber sighed. Great, just great. Her cousin was so soused that even if she told her what was wrong, Celia wouldn't remember it tomorrow. "I think you ought to get to bed. Here," she extended her hand. "Grab on, I'll pull you up."

"That's damned sweet of you." She grabbed Amber's hand and pulled herself up. Grunting, she swayed ever so slightly as she got to her feet.

Still holding on to Celia's hand, Amber helped her down the short hallway to her bedroom.

"Thanks," Celia said. She burped. "I think I can make it from here. Gooo night . . ."

"Good night," Amber murmured. She went back to her own room and flopped down onto the bed. Well, great. What was she going to do now?

Amber sighed. She'd do what she'd been doing since her mom died. She'd handle it on her own.

But by the next morning, she'd changed her mind. Why should she have to deal with this alone, she asked herself as she headed down the hall to the kitchen. Celia was taking plenty of money from the estate to be her guardian, darn it. So let her earn some of it.

Celia was leaning against the counter, staring at the coffee machine. "Come on," she muttered. "Hurry up . . . hurry up . . ."

"Morning, Celia," Amber said loudly. "I'm glad you're up so early. I need to talk to you."

Celia put her hands over her ears. "Shush. Not so loud. My head hurts."

"There's a surprise," Amber said brightly. "But headache or not, we've got to talk."

"Can't it wait till later," Celia moaned. "I'm in no shape to listen."

"It has already waited long enough." Amber folded her arms over her chest, refusing to be put off. "And this is really important."

Celia sighed dramatically. "Okay, let me pour my coffee."

Amber flopped down at the table and waited until Celia, moving at a snail's pace, finally pulled out the opposite chair and sat down. "Okay, shoot," she muttered. "What's so darned important?"

"This guy at school's been harassing me. He's ticked off that I wouldn't let him copy my quiz paper and he's been bullying me ever since. So far, he's threatened me, written disgusting things on my locker and tried to run me over with his car."

Celia gaped at her. "Are you kidding? He tried to run you over?"

"Do I sound like I'm kidding?" Amber asked.

"How come you waited so long to tell me all this?" Celia took a sip from her coffee.

"I've been trying to tell you. You always say you're too busy to listen."

Celia's eyes narrowed. "When? When did you say something? I don't remember us talking about this."

"Last week," Amber replied. She wondered why Celia was getting so defensive. "The first time I tried, you accused me of eavesdropping on your private conversation and the second time, you said you were busy. It was the time you and Dale were on your way out to play miniature golf."

"You should have been more persistent," Celia protested. "If I'd known you were having so much trouble, I'd have done something about it." She paused for a moment and took a deep breath. "Uh, you haven't said anything to Mr. Lindstrom, have you?"

"Mr. Lindstrom?" Amber repeated. "No. Why would I? He's an estate lawyer."

Celia nodded. "Good, then, uh, we don't want to bother him with something trivial like this."

"I don't call being harassed and bullied trivial."

"No, no, of course not," Celia said. "I meant that there's no need to bring him into this. I'll take care of it myself. I'll call the school today."

"I've already spoken to the vice principal, Mr. Mullins." Amber got to her feet. She picked up her backpack off the counter and slung it over her shoulder. "He was supposed to talk to Jack."

"Is that the kid that's bugging you?"

"Yeah. His name is Jack Redden and he's in my fourth-period history class. Make sure you mention that to Mr. Mullins. And be sure to tell him that we're going to hold the school responsible if something happens to me."

Celia blinked in surprise. "You're that scared?"

"Of course I'm scared. Redden's a lunatic. Worse, he's a lunatic with rich parents and a car. Remember that when you talk to the school. You'll have to get tough, tell them you're holding them responsible for my safety."

"Do you think that'll work?" Celia asked. "From what I remember of high school, the administration was pretty useless."

"Well, they'd better do something." Amber sighed. "I can't go on like this. I'm tired of watching my back all the time. I'd better hurry if I'm going to make my bus. Oh, by the way, I think I will be calling Mr. Lindstrom."

"But I said I'd take care of this," Celia interrupted angrily.

"I want to talk to him about learning to drive," Amber said. Jeez, her cousin was sure jumpy. "He's the one holding the purse strings, remember. He's got to authorize putting out the cash for lessons."

"Oh, that." Celia looked visibly relieved. "Don't bother. I've already talked to him. He sent some extra money with the last check. It's for driving lessons."

"Why didn't you tell me?" Amber was confused. "We got our checks last week."

Celia shrugged. "I meant to, I just forgot. But that's not important. I'll call the driving school and make the arrangements. Do you have any preference about when you want to take the lessons?"

"Any time will be fine." Amber glanced at the clock on the stove. "I'm going to miss the bus if I don't get moving. Will you be here this evening?"

Celia looked away. "Uh, Dale and I are going out to dinner. But I'll be home early."

"Okay, I'll see you tonight."

After school, Amber made it to the bus stop with about ten seconds to spare. Brandon was already there. They climbed on board and took their usual seats in the back. She closed her eyes briefly. She'd been edgy all day at school. Every time she'd walked down a hallway she half expected Jack Redden to leap out at her. But nothing had happened. During history, she glanced at him once over her shoulder and he wasn't paying any attention to her at all. By the time school was out and she was on the bus home, she let herself relax. Between herself and Celia complaining to Mr. Mullins, maybe he'd actually done something. The thought made her smile.

"What are you ginning about?" Brandon asked.

Amber turned and looked at him. "Nothing, I'm just glad the day is over."

"You got plans for the evening?" he asked. He pulled off his sunglasses and tucked them in his top pocket.

"Nope. I'm just going swimming and then studying for tomorrow's history test."

"I wish we had a pool," Brandon said.

Amber hesitated. She wasn't sure if she was allowed to have friends over or not. "Uh, would you like to come over and swim?"

"I'd love to." He grinned. "But I can't today. I promised my mom I'd help her clean out the garage. How about tomorrow?"

"That's no good." Amber shook her head. "There won't be time. I'm going to the football game."

"You're a football fan?" He looked surprised.

"Nah, but I'd like to see one before I get out of high school," she explained. She gave him a brief explanation of how she'd spent the last few years taking care of her mother. "I'm going with Harriet and her friend Mark . . ."

"Harriet Islington?" he interrupted. "I know her— we've got honors English together. I didn't know you were friends. She's a nice girl. I've always wanted to get to know her better."

"Why don't you come with us?" Amber invited. "We're going out for burgers afterward. It'll be fun."

Brandon hesitated. "You sure it'd be cool with them?"

"It's cool. None of us are exactly cheerleader types. We're all going for the same reason—we've never been to one before. So no one's going to take the game seriously. Come on, it'll be fun. The more the merrier. Right?"

"Right. Okay." He whipped out a pen and paper. "Here's my phone number. Call me with the details. You want to meet at school or what?"

"I think Mark is going to drive," she said. "But it'll be easier if you come to my place. Is that okay?"

"That's cool. I don't live that far from you."

The bus pulled up at her stop. Amber scrambled to her feet. "I'll call you tonight after I talk to Harriet," she said as she hurried to the back door. She waved to him as the vehicle pulled away.

Amber stood on the curb for a few seconds before stepping into the street. She looked both ways. The road was empty. There was no sign of a black Beemer anywhere. She crossed the street and headed for the entrance to the mobile home park.

The trailer was silent. Amber tossed her backpack on the couch and then went into the kitchen to flip on the air-conditioning. One thing Celia wasn't cranky about was running the air. She liked the place to stay cool. Amber opened the fridge, pulled out a soda and then headed to her room to change into her bathing suit.

A few minutes later, she was ready. She poured the rest of the soda into a big plastic cup, grabbed her towel and keys and headed out the door.

The pool was in a fenced enclave at the end of their street. Amber unlocked the gate and went inside. She was delighted to see that she had the place to herself. The pool area was really nice. Bright, blue-and-white striped umbrellas provided shade for the tables dotting the patio area. At the far end was a Jacuzzi.

She put her cup down on a table, stepped out of her thongs and took off her oversized shirt. Walking to the edge, she stuck her toe in and made a face. Compared to the air temperature, it felt cool. Taking a deep breath, Amber plunged straight in. The water shocked her silly but she loved it. She surfaced a moment later, giggling and gasping for air. Tossing her hair out of her eyes, she flopped backward, kicked her legs and began doing back rolls in the water. Then she did front rolls and handstands. She came out of her last handstand and flattened out, intending to do laps. She froze. She was not alone—a shadow blocked the sun.

Squinting, she saw Chris Bartlett standing at the edge of the pool watching her. "Hi." He grinned widely. "You look like you were having a good time."

"I was." She smiled weakly. "I thought I was alone."

"You mind if I join you?"

As he was wearing red-and-black surfer trunks and had a towel slung around his shoulders, Amber was pretty sure that he'd join her whether she minded or not. Not that she did. She was simply embarrassed to have been caught playing like a ten-year-old kid.

"Not at all, come on in, the water's nice. Uh, especially on such a hot day." Darn, now she was starting to babble. She clamped her mouth shut and tried not to notice how incredibly good he looked.

His skin was tanned a glorious shade of bronzy brown, his chest had filled out past that awkward lanky boy stage and his smile was perfect. Amber caught herself staring and quickly looked away. She wished she'd worn her new suit. But she'd thrown on this old navy blue tank suit because she'd been too lazy to dig her new one out of the top of her closet.

He tossed the towel onto a nearby chair and dived into the deep end. Amber, feeling stupid, stayed where she was. She wasn't sure what to do. She hadn't had a lot of experience with guys in situations like this. But she wanted to be cool. She wanted to be sophisticated and most of all, she didn't want to make a fool of herself.

Chris cut through the water and surfaced a foot in front of her. "That felt good."

"Yeah, it's nice on a hot day like today." She cringed as she realized she was repeating herself. How lame could she get? "Uh, you swim here often?" She cringed again as the words left her mouth. That sounded like the worst sort of pick-up line, like something from a bad seventies TV show.

"Yup," he said. As he was a lot taller than she, the water, which was up to her chest, only came up to his waist. "We've got a pool at home, but I spend a lot of time here with my grandmother."

Amber hadn't noticed him being around much, but she wasn't going to argue the point. "That's nice of you. Your grandma's a great person. She's been really good to me since I moved in."

"She's told me all about you," he said.

"Good things, I hope." Amber laughed.

"She likes you." He grinned. "She said everyone here was kinda worried when they heard you were moving in . . ."

"Why? This isn't a senior citizens' park."

He shrugged. "Not officially, but except for your cousin and a couple of other people, that's mainly who lives here. And your cousin's gone most of the time."

"Yeah." Amber's smile faded. "I know."

"You want a Coke or something?" Chris started for the edge of the pool. There was a soft drink vending machine by the water fountain.

"That'd be great," she replied.

While Chris got the drinks, Amber climbed out of the pool, toweled off and sat down at one of the big, round tables.

"Here." He plopped the can down in front of her and then leaned up to adjust the umbrella. "Let's move this so the sun's not in our eyes."

"Thanks," Amber said gratefully.

Chris sat down and chugged back his soda. "So," he said, "how do you like Lansdale High?"

"It's okay," she replied. "But it's kind of hard having to start a new school in your senior year."

"That's tough," he agreed. "Grandma told me what happened, I mean, how you ended up here." He looked away briefly and then back at her. When their eyes met, his were sympathetic. "I'm sorry about your mom. It must have really been the pits, losing her like that."

Tears welled up in her eyes. "It was," she said

softly. "She was the best mom in the world. We were so close. There'd just been the two of us, you know."

"What happened to your dad?" he asked quietly.

"He died when I was little." She swallowed hard to get the lump out of her throat. Sometimes, she could forget how alone in the world she really was. Sometimes.

"I'm sorry, I shouldn't be asking such nosy questions." He reached across and laid his hand on hers.

"No, it's okay," she said quickly. "I'm fine, really."

"I shoulda kept my big mouth shut." He shook his head in disgust. "Here I've been trying to meet you and when I finally do, I blow it big-time with a bunch of dumb questions that aren't any of my business anyhow."

He'd been trying to meet her? Amber couldn't believe her ears. Wow, no one had ever tried to meet her before. She was incredibly flattered. "No, it's okay, really. I'm acting like a baby, that's all. It's been a lousy week at school. Besides, I like talking about her. That's part of the trouble . . . my mom passed away and then a few weeks later I was down here. I never really got a chance to talk about her to anyone and she was so great."

"What about your cousin?"

Amber didn't want to bad-mouth Celia. "She didn't really know my mom." Tears sprang back into her eyes and she swiped at them furiously. "I'm sorry. I'm acting like a baby. I'm fine now. I hope I haven't embarrassed you."

"Hey, don't worry about it. I understand." He

pulled back and stared at her closely. "You sure you're okay?"

"I'm sure." She smiled warmly. "And it's nice of you to say you wanted to meet me. I have to admit, it's been tough lately. This may not sound cool, but it gets kinda lonely when you're the new kid on the block."

"Tough, man, sounds to me like it's been a little worse than that." He took another drink of his soda. "Have you made any friends at school yet?"

"A few." She rubbed her finger against the cold soda can. "We're going to a football game tomorrow night. I've never been to one before so it should be fun."

"Do you know much about the game?"

"No."

He laughed. "Cool, then you'll have a good time. If you want, I can tell you the rules. I used to play a little."

"That'd be great." He could talk about football or anything else as long as he stayed.

For the next hour, Chris and Amber talked like they were old friends. He told her a little about football and she told him about the things she liked: reading and movies. She was delighted to find that both of them were film buffs and that Chris was an avid reader, too.

"Wow," he exclaimed, "you've read *Watchers*, that's one of my favorite books. Dean Koontz can really spin a yarn."

"His books grab you from the first page," she agreed, "and he keeps you hooked until the end. I love suspense. The scarier the better."

"Same here." His gaze shifted as he looked past

Amber toward the gate. "Here comes Grandma. Uh, I guess I've got to go."

Amber was disappointed that their time was ending. Chris was so easy to talk to.

"Yoo-hoo, Chris," Lucy yelled. "It's getting late. We've got to go. Your mom's meeting us at the restaurant."

"I'll be right there," Chris called to her.

"Ask Amber if she wants to come with us." Lucy's voice was loud enough to wake the dead. "The more the merrier, right!"

Amber cringed. Talk about embarrassing. Granny was really putting poor Chris in a hot spot. "You don't have to invite me," she said softly. "Lucy's just being nice."

"I'd love for you to come." He grinned. "We're talking dinner with my mom and Grandma. That isn't exactly the most exciting night of the year. Don't get me wrong, they're cool and all, but they are family. We have a good time, but it'll be even better if you come along. Please?"

"Are you sure?" She hesitated. "I don't want to barge in or intrude."

"You're not intruding. We want you to come. Come on, say you'll go."

"Do I have time to get ready?" Amber glanced toward the gate. Lucy was walking back toward her house.

"You've got plenty of time. Grandma always starts fussing way too early." He grinned broadly. "Her generation thinks being five minutes late is one of the seven deadly sins."

Amber realized that if she didn't go, she'd spend another evening eating a frozen dinner in front of the television. She was pretty darned sick of that. As a matter of fact, she was so sick of eating alone she'd have accepted an invitation from the Three Stooges. "Well, if you're sure it's okay with your mom, then I'd love to go. Give me fifteen minutes to throw on some clothes."

Amber took the world's fastest shower. She threw on a pale green summer dress, grabbed her purse and flew down the hall to the living room. Grabbing a pen and a pad of Post-it paper off the top of the table by the phone, she scribbled a note telling Celia where she was going and what time she'd be home.

She slapped the note on the front of the television and turned for the front door. The phone rang and she made a dive for it. "Hello."

There was no answer.

Frowning, she gave the handset a shake. "Hello." She raised her voice slightly. The phone was an older model and she didn't think the wiring was all that great.

From the other end of the line, she heard a faint noise. She wasn't sure, but it sounded like a giggle. Oh great, a crank call. "Hello," she repeated. "Is there anyone there?"

"Hee . . . hee . . . hee . . ."

She jerked back as laughter burst through the wires. Even holding the phone away from her ear, she could hear the mocking, ugly sound. Geez, she thought, whoever it was sounded like a serial killer in a teenage slasher flick.

"Who is this?" Amber demanded. She'd crank-called a few times herself as a kid. It was only fun if you got a reaction out of the person on the other end. She'd play along for a minute or two.

"Ha . . . ha . . . ha . . ."

"This isn't funny, you know," she said, forcing her voice to stay stern. She grinned as she thought of the kids on the other end of the line trying to hold back their giggles.

"Oh, yes it is." The voice was a mere whisper. It was impossible to tell if it was a boy or a girl. "And it's going to get even funnier, Amber. Just wait and see."

Amber's smile disappeared. This was no crank call. Whoever it was knew her name. Fear snaked up her spine. "Who is this?"

This time, the caller said nothing.

"Who is this?" she yelled.

"Your worst nightmare."

"I'm calling the police," she cried. She was suddenly, absolutely sure she knew what was going on here. "Is that you, Redden? If it is, you're in big trouble. They can trace calls, you know. This kind of harassment isn't just school bullying, it's against the law. This is stalking . . ." It took a moment before she realized she was talking to empty air.

Her tormentor had hung up.

There was a knock on the front door. Amber jumped.

"Hey, Amber," Chris yelled. "You ready yet?"

"Just a sec." She took a deep, steadying breath. She

didn't want to let on that anything was wrong. Especially not in front of Chris's mother and grandmother. Or for that matter, in front of Chris. Lucy might understand, but Amber had a feeling she'd sound like a real neurotic mess if she let on that she thought she was being stalked. She wasn't a celebrity or anything.

She grabbed her purse, smoothed her hair back and went to the door. "Hi." She plastered a cheerful smile on her face as she stepped outside.

Chris's eyes widened appreciatively. "You look good."

"Thanks," she replied. "I hope I didn't keep you waiting."

"You didn't."

Lucy came out her front door. She was wearing a wild pink, orange and green sundress, a giant straw hat and oversized dark glasses. "I'm starving," she said as she joined them on the pavement. "I could eat a horse. Where are we meeting Marta? I hope it ain't one of those sushi restaurants like your dad dragged us to last week. Can't imagine why anyone wants to eat raw fish. Not that I mind what others want to eat, but I'd just as soon sink my teeth into real cooked food." She looked at Chris as she spoke.

He laughed. "You're safe, Grandma. We're meeting Mom at Harbingers. I know it's kind of a teenage hangout, but they have really good food. Especially the burgers and fries."

"Thank goodness," Lucy said fervently.

"Is that okay with you?" Chris asked Amber. "You're not a vegetarian or anything, are you?"

"Nope. I love burgers."

"Good. Come on, then. Let's get going." He pointed toward the parking area by the pool. "My car's over there."

She took another long, deep breath as she fell into step with the other two. Amber hoped her face didn't give her away. That phone call had given her a bad case of the willies.

Her heart was still pounding like a jackhammer and even in the warm evening air cold sweat beaded on the back of her neck. But she must look okay, she thought, because neither Chris nor Lucy was staring at her or anything like that.

But something was wrong. Very wrong. She had an awful feeling that it was only going to get worse. Amber told herself not to overreact, that it was just a phone call. But it had shaken her badly.

She hoped that Celia would keep her promise and do something about it.

Chapter
Five

Dear Diary,
This has been a crazy, crazy day and it's not over yet.
Now I'm waiting for Celia to get home so I can find
out if she really did keep her promise.

Dinner was great. Chris's mom is really nice. She
went out of her way to make me feel welcome. Chris is
cool, too. I mean, I'd like to go out with him. But we'll
have to see if he's really interested or if he's just killing
time. I don't know where this is going. He did ask for
my phone number. That's a good sign.

Speaking of calls, the one I got before we went to
dinner freaked me out. I know it was Jack; it had to be.
No one else hates me. How could they? I haven't been
here long enough to make that many enemies. Just
Jack. I still don't know what it is about me that
punches his buttons. Give me a break, I can't be the
first person who wouldn't let him cheat on a quiz.

*Celia promised she'd call the school . . . maybe
that's why Jack tried the phone thing. Maybe he got
called into the office and was told to leave me alone.
Maybe I'm grasping at straws, too. Somehow, I don't
have a lot of faith in my cousin. I hope she proves me
wrong. I'm going to pray Celia handled it and that she
let the school know we're serious. But I don't know
what I can do if they ignore her, too.*

Amber looked up as she heard the jingle of keys in
the front door. "Celia?" she called. She shoved her
diary aside and stood up. "Celia? Is that you?"

"Yeah," her cousin yelled back.

Amber hurried into the living room. "Hi, did you
have a nice evening?"

Celia blew a strand of hair off her face and tossed
her purse on the couch. "Yeah, we had a good time."
She kicked off her high-heeled sling-back shoes. "We
went to that steak house over on First Street. Is there
anything to drink? Dale's air-conditioning packed up
and I'm burning up."

"There's soda and juice in the fridge."

Celia headed in that direction. Amber was right on
her heels.

"Uh, did you call the school today?"

Celia opened the refrigerator and stuck her head inside. "I don't see any soda . . ."

"It's in the door on the bottom shelf," Amber said
impatiently. "What did they say when you talked to
them?"

"What did who say?" Celia had a can of root beer in
her hand when she emerged. She closed the door,

leaned back, popped the top on the can and took a long swig.

"The school." Amber's hands clenched into fists. Darn, she knew this was going to happen. Celia hadn't done anything. If she had, she wouldn't be trying so hard not to answer any questions. "When you called them and told them I was being stalked . . ."

"Stalked?" Celia laughed. "Don't you think you're being a bit melodramatic?"

"No," Amber replied bluntly. "And neither would you if he was making your life miserable. It happened again this afternoon."

"That kid came here?" Celia asked harshly.

"He called me. You know, like it was a crank call. Only it was him. I know it was him. No one else would be that obnoxious."

"Did he threaten you?"

"I've already told you. Jack isn't that dumb. He never actually threatens me." Amber was getting tired of this. She'd told everyone a dozen times that he was too clever to be specific about what he was going to do to her. "But he implies I'd better watch out. That something terrible is going to happen. Look, did you call the school or not? More important, are they going to do anything about it?"

"I told you I'd call and I did." Celia took another sip and went toward the living room. "They said they'd talk to this boy. Tell him to leave you alone."

"Who did you talk to?"

"The vice principal, some guy named Mullins." Celia flopped down on the couch and reached for the remote control. She punched the power button and the

TV flickered to life. "You want to watch *Letterman* with me?"

"No thanks." Amber sighed. What had she expected? That Celia would go down there and make a scene? That she actually cared enough to go out of her way? Fat chance. "Did he take you seriously? Did he understand we expect him to do something about Jack?"

"He told me he thought you were overreacting." Celia's gaze was focused on the TV screen. "That losing your mom and having to move to a new school had upset you more than you're willing to admit. I don't know, he started talking a bunch of that psychological mumbo jumbo—on and on about this and that and losing a loved one . . ."

"Of course losing Mom upset me," Amber interrupted. "It would upset anyone. But that doesn't mean I'm overreacting about being harassed. That's what he told me when I saw him, too. He tried to make it seem like there was something wrong with me."

Celia shrugged. "I finally told the old fart I didn't care whether you were overreacting or not. You weren't the problem. Jack Redden's the problem. If he and the board of education knew what's good for them, they'd make damned sure that this loony kid stays the hell away from you."

Surprised, Amber said, "You did?" Maybe she was wrong. Maybe Celia did care.

"Yup. Oh, look, there's that Chihuahua, the one that does all those taco commercials. I thing he's so cute." She glanced up at Amber and smiled wanly. "You sure you don't want to watch some TV?"

"No, thanks, I've got to go to school tomorrow."
Amber smiled back at her. She was strangely touched
by her cousin's faith in her. Besides, maybe Celia's
bluntness with old Mullins was enough to get him off
his duff to do something about Redden. "But thanks
for asking."

"You want me to call the phone company tomorrow?" Celia asked.

"The phone company? Why?"

Celia cocked her head to one side and studied her
closely. "Didn't you just tell me that kid called here
today? That he was threatening you?"

"Oh, yeah, but, I mean, uh, what can the phone
company do? They're not going to tap the phone or put
a tracer on the line or anything like that, are they?"
Amber was genuinely confused.

"Hardly. We're not talking the crime of the century
here." Celia rolled her eyes. "But they will change the
number."

Amber felt like a fool. "I should have thought of
that. Uh, wouldn't that be a lot of trouble for you? I
mean, you'd have to give all your friends your new
number . . ."

"If that's what we've got to do, that's what we've
got to do." Celia yawned. "I've had crazy ex-
boyfriends crank-call me. It ain't fun and it sure as
heck ain't funny."

Amber thought about it for a moment. "Thanks for
being so understanding, Celia. But no, I don't want to
change our phone number. That'd be too much like letting him win."

"I'll get a whistle and put it by the phone," Celia

said. "One of those really good ones, you know, like soccer coaches use."

"A whistle?"

"Sure." Celia grinned broadly. "The next time the idiot calls, blast the whistle into the mouthpiece. His ears will be ringing for a week. And he'll think twice before he does it again."

"You sound like you know what you're talking about." Amber laughed.

"I do." Celia giggled. "Like I said, I've had crazy ex-boyfriends. Sometimes a girl just has to prove that the phone can be her friend."

Amber deliberately waited until a few seconds before the tardy bell before walking into her history class. As she slid into her seat, she looked back at Redden. He gave her a sneering smile in return.

She turned her attention to the front of the class. The bell rang and Mr. Powers put down his newspaper. "We're going to have a quiz," he announced.

There was a collective groan from the class. Powers was unfazed. He picked up a stack of papers from the corner of the desk and began passing them out to the people in the first row. "Pass these back," he instructed. "You'll have fifteen minutes to complete the quiz and then we'll exchange papers and grade them here in class. It'll give you a chance to see how you're doing."

Amber took a sheet off the top and handed the rest of them behind her. She whipped out her pen and got started. The test was easy, provided, of course, you'd done the homework and read the textbook chapters.

Amber had done both, so she whizzed through it in record time. She sat back and waited until the time was up.

"Time's up," Mr. Powers called. "Everyone pass their paper to the person on their right. You kids in the last row, pass your papers to the front and I'll distribute them to the first row. As soon as we've done that, we'll go over the questions one at a time and I'll write the answers on the board."

It took a few minutes to get organized, but finally Mr. Powers was up at the front of the class, scribbling away on the blackboard. When they'd finished the last question, he put down the chalk and came toward the first row. "Okay, write the number of incorrect answers on the top of the page, circle it, and pass the papers back to their owners. Put the quiz on my desk on your way out. I know it was only a quiz, but this is an honors class and the grade counts. First row, pass those papers back to me."

Amber smiled at Julie Steadman as she reached for her quiz paper. She gasped when she saw the bright bold number circled at the top. Ten! She couldn't believe it. This was a twenty-question quiz and she'd missed over half. No way.

She studied her sheet carefully. Wait a minute, this couldn't be right, she thought. Someone had crossed out the answer she'd originally circled on the multiple choice questions and recircled the wrong answer. Quickly, she scanned the other missed questions. They were all the same. Her correct answer was crossed out and the incorrect one circled. She looked across the aisle. Julie was watching her out of the corner of her eye.

"What's going on?" Amber held out the paper. "How dare you change my answers?"

"I don't know what you're talking about," she mumbled.

"The heck you don't," Amber yelped. Just then the bell rang. Julie scrambled to her feet, snatched her pack and flew toward Mr. Powers's desk.

"Hey," Amber yelled. She leapt to her feet and charged after her. "Wait!"

"Is there a problem here?" Mr. Powers asked. He stared at the two girls.

"I don't have a problem." Julie shrugged casually. She dropped her quiz on Mr. Powers's desk. "I just want to get to my next class. That girl"—she jerked her head toward Amber—"seems to think I did something to her paper. I don't know what she's talking about."

Amber realized the entire class was staring at them. She also realized that it was her word against Julie's. Julie who dated the kid on the football team; Julie who was a cheerleader . . . darn. Amber didn't want to make any more enemies. She was far enough ahead grade-wise that she could afford to flunk a quiz. Especially in this class. She'd already done an extra credit project.

"Amber," Mr. Powers said, "what's this all about?"

"It's nothing." Amber stepped back toward her desk and picked up her backpack. By this time the other students had started getting out of their seats. She picked up her quiz paper, walked back to the teacher's desk and slapped it on top of Julie's. "There's nothing wrong, Mr. Powers. I made a mistake. That's all."

He nodded distractedly. His gaze had already shifted to the unread sports section of the newspaper.

Amber hurried out of the class.

"What was that all about?" Harriet asked as she caught up with her. The girls headed across the quad.

"That girl changed my answers on the quiz," she replied.

"Julie did that?" Harriet blinked in surprise. "You're kidding. Why? I mean, she's one of the rah-rah cheerleader types, but what's she got against you?"

"Nothing." Amber shrugged. "I mean, I've never done anything to her."

"She really likes John Berry. Maybe she's still ticked off because he changed seats with you," Harriet suggested.

"Maybe."

"Did you tell Mr. Powers?"

Amber hesitated. "I started to, then I realized the whole darned class was staring at me and that it would be my word against hers."

"So?"

"So." Amber wasn't sure she could explain it. "So she's a popular girl. I haven't exactly been a big hit in Mr. Powers's class. I didn't want to tick anyone else off. I mean, I'm not going to let anyone intimidate me, but I thought I'd talk to her first before I raised a fuss."

Harriet nodded. "That's probably a good idea. But honestly, there isn't any legitimate reason for her to change your answers. I'd be furious if someone did that to me."

"There's Mark." Amber waved at their friend. "I think he wants us to hurry."

"Hey, get the lead out." Mark jingled a set of keys from his fingers. "Come on, I've got wheels today. We can go get some burgers!"

By the time school was out and Amber was home, she'd pushed the incident with the quiz paper out of her mind. What was the point? Even if she cornered the cheerleader, the girl would lie. But the whole ugly thing rankled. Amber decided she'd let it go this time. If something else happened, she'd raise a ruckus. Besides, she told herself as she rummaged through her top drawer, today had gone okay. Jack had left her alone.

It looked like Celia's phone call had made a difference. Amber found her black tank top at the very bottom of the drawer. Taking it out, she pulled it on and then stepped back and examined her reflection in the full-length mirror on the back of her door.

She smiled at her reflection. She wasn't vain, but the top went perfectly with the fitted jeans and the black wedge sandals. She added a delicate gold necklace and then dabbed a little of her favorite perfume behind her ears.

She went out to the living room. It was almost seven and Celia wasn't home yet. Amber hastily scribbled a note telling her cousin where she was going and when she expected to be home. "I don't know why I'm bothering," she muttered to herself as she slapped the paper onto the television screen, "Celia sure as anything will be out later than I will." But old habits die hard and Amber still left the note. Her mom had trained her well—always let someone know where you're going and when you'll be back.

At two minutes to the hour, she grabbed her purse, locked the door behind her and hurried out to the main road. She'd cleared the main entrance when Mark and Harriet drove up.

Mark's car was a four-door Toyota. She climbed in the backseat. "Hi."

"I thought Brandon Yates was coming," Mark said.

"He's meeting us at the game," Amber replied. "He had to help his mom do something."

"Hi." Harriet smiled over her shoulder at Amber. "Wow. You look good."

"Hey, don't I look good?" Mark demanded.

"You're wearing the same clothes you had on at school," Amber pointed out. She grinned at Harriet. "And you look great, too. What happened to your glasses?"

"I'm wearing contacts."

"When did you get them?" Amber asked.

"A couple of weeks ago." Harriet smiled shyly. "I'm, uh, kind of a wuss when it comes to putting them in, so I've had to build up my tolerance time real slow. I'm finally at the point where I can wear them for a whole evening."

"You look fabulous," Amber enthused. "And I love your hair like that."

Harriet had let her dark brown curls hang loose around her face instead of pulling them back in a rubber band. Without the glasses and with the new hairstyle, she looked really, really pretty. She was even wearing makeup.

"I like it down, too," Mark added. "I'm trying to talk her into wearing it that way all the time, but Harriet is one stubborn girl."

"You should," Amber agreed. "It really looks great!"

"I don't know," Harriet said doubtfully. "It's a lot more trouble to take care of then just pulling it back."

"Think about it, okay?" Amber pressed. "You really look fabulous. The hair frames your features perfectly."

"Hey, be careful. You don't want to give the girl a big head." Mark said.

"Like yours." Harriet poked him in the ribs.

They laughed and teased each other all the way to school. Mark pulled his car into the line waiting to get into the parking lot behind the stadium where Lansdale High played their home football games.

In the warm evening, they had their windows rolled down. So did everyone else and the air was filled with the sound of rock music from various stations. They were making the turn into the parking lot when there was a loud squeal of brakes and a black car shot past them. The car almost ploughed into a Mazda truck, slammed on the brakes and then fishtailed to the right, avoiding a collision at the last minute. The driver of the Mazda stuck his head out, made an obscene gesture and yelled, but by this time the black car had pulled around the row of stopped cars and disappeared.

"Guess he didn't want to wait in line," Harriet commented with a nervous giggle.

"Why should he? The great Jack Redden isn't like the rest of us." Mark's tone was disgusted. "Jeez, one of these days someone's gonna pop that guy one and I hope I'm around to see it."

"Me, too," Amber said. She hoped she wouldn't run into Redden tonight. She glanced nervously at Mark and Harriet; she didn't want to get her friends involved in her hassles.

Mark found a parking space and they all piled out. Walking across the unpaved parking lot, Amber noted that a lot of kids did double takes when they realized that Harriet was Harriet. As they stood in line to buy their tickets to the game, Amber noticed a tall, good-looking Asian boy staring at Harriet. She poked her in the arm. "Don't look now, but you've got an admirer."

"Who?" Harriet's head whipped around. "Where?"

"I said not to look," Amber hissed. "It's that Asian guy standing about ten people behind us."

"I know who you mean." Harriet smiled widely. "That's Tom Chang. We've got physics together. He's really smart."

"Yeah and it looks to me like he's really horny, too," Mark interjected. He glared in Tom's direction. "Jeez, his tongue's practically hanging out."

Harriet laughed. "Really? I mean, you're kidding, right?"

Mark raised an eyebrow. "No, I'm not kidding. How do you see yourself? As the bride of Frankenstein or something? Come on, Harri baby, you're one good-looking chickie . . ."

Both the girls groaned.

"I thought 'chickie' went out with the seventies," Amber said with a laugh. She could see that behind Mark's teasing manner, he was dead serious. He was also crazy about Harriet. She wondered why she hadn't noticed before. Tom Chang had competition.

Maybe it was because she'd been too wrapped up in her own problems to notice.

"I didn't know that 'chickie' was ever in," Harriet said with a laugh. She punched Mark playfully in the arm. "But thanks for the compliment. Keep talking like that and maybe I'll buy you a box of popcorn."

"You'll have to take me to the movies for that; they don't sell popcorn here," Mark replied.

"Sounds good to me."

"You want to go tomorrow night?" Mark tried to sound casual. "There're some good flicks playing now."

Harriet hesitated. "Well, I don't know . . ."

Mark's hopeful expression vanished. "It's okay, I understand. You've probably got other plans . . ."

"Kinda. I mean, I was going to ask you guys to come over tomorrow night." She shrugged. "It's no big deal. My parents are going out and they said I could have a few friends over if I swore on a stack of Bibles that we wouldn't drink or smoke grass or have wild orgies on the patio."

They'd worked their way toward the front of the line. Mark dug out his wallet and pulled out a twenty. "That sounds great," he said enthusiastically. "I guess that means you don't want me showing up with a six-pack of Bud or a bottle of wine in a brown paper bag."

"Very funny." Harriet whipped open her purse and pulled out a small red change purse. Taking out a five, she handed it to Mark. "Here, get my ticket, too."

Amber dug her own cash out. "Mine, too."

Mark waved them both away. "Forget it, ladies. Tonight's on me. You two can buy the burgers."

"Okay." That sounded good to Amber.

They got their tickets and went into the stands. "Can we sit up there?" Amber pointed to the very top. The bleachers were empty up there but she was sure the view would be great.

"Considering that none of us know diddly about the game, it doesn't matter where we sit," Mark said. He grabbed Harriet's hand and they started up the steep stairs.

"I know how it's played," Amber said as she fell into step behind them. She looked around, hoping to spot Brandon.

"You didn't know how it was played two days ago," Harriet said over her shoulder. "What'd you do, read up on it? I think that's taking school spirit a step too far. Jeez, Amber, even I'm not that big of a geek."

"I didn't read a book, my neighbor's good-looking grandson told me the rules."

Harriet's head whipped around. She stumbled on the next step, but Mark's grip kept her from falling. "Oops! Your neighbor had a good-looking grandson?"

"Yup. He's really cute and he asked me for my phone number."

They'd reached the top. They turned into the center section and made their way to the middle. Mark plunked himself down and patted a spot on either side

of him. "Have a seat. I've decided that in the interests
of humanity, I'll share myself with both of you. I
wouldn't want to be the cause of bloodshed because
two lovely ladies came to blows over who could sit
next to me."

"Oh, please." Amber groaned.

"I think I'm going to throw up," Harriet said.

Mark laughed. "You know it's true. You just don't
want to admit it. But go on, say it. You both want me."

"So tell me about this good-looking guy who asked
for your phone number." Harriet looked past Mark to
Amber.

Amber was suddenly self-conscious. Maybe having
a guy ask for your phone number was no big deal.
Maybe she'd made too much of it. "He's really nice.
His name is Chris. He graduated from Lansdale last
year."

"Chris who?" Mark asked.

"Chris Bartlett."

"Wow. You probably do know something about
football if he was your teacher."

"He said he used to play a little," Amber replied.

"A little?" Mark threw back his head and laughed.
"He was Lansdale's star player. He could have made
all-state but he injured his leg right before our last
play-off game. He's a pretty decent guy, too."

"He's really nice," Amber said.

Harriet was staring at her speculatively. "I know
him, too. We had honors chemistry together last year.
So, he asked for your phone number, huh?"

Amber sighed. "Well, yeah, but . . . but . . . okay, he
said he wanted it so he could call me if he got worried

about his grandmother. I'm sorry, you guys, I kinda made it sound like he asked for my number so he could ask for a date."

"Nah." Harriet smiled sympathetically. "You didn't make it sound like that."

"Yes, I did." Amber laughed. "I didn't really mean to . . . well, I guess I did."

"Hey, stop beating yourself up." Mark slapped her on the back. "Besides, I'll bet all that talk about worrying about his grandmother is just a clever ploy . . ." He dropped his voice conspiratorially. "He only used it to get your number so he could ask you out. Trust me, I know guys. I know how their minds work and you are one beautiful chickie."

Amber and Harriet both laughed. Then Amber spotted Brandon. "There he is. I was wondering if he was going to make it on time." She and Harriet both began to wave. Brandon saw them and started for the top.

"You guys like the nosebleed section?" he asked with a wide grin as he reached them

"Amber picked the spot," Mark said. "She was afraid she'd miss something."

Brandon plopped down next to her. For once, he wasn't wearing shades. "Cool. Now that I'm here, does anyone know anything about this game?"

"Just yell when Amber does," Mark teased. "She's our resident expert."

"Jeez, what a bunch of nerds," Amber shot back with a laugh. "Oh look, here come the players."

Lansdale was playing one of their arch rivals, Wilson High. The crowd went wild with cheers and whistles as the teams took the field.

The game was exciting. Amber enjoyed herself enormously. She loved everything about the evening. The crisp chill that nipped in the air as the night lengthened. The slight swell of ground fog that rose from the grass and the scent of hot dogs and french fries wafting through the stands. At halftime, Lansdale was up by seven points. The bands of both high schools each performed a couple of tunes and then the game started up again. By the time the final whistle blew, Lansdale had won by two touchdowns.

Afterward, they went to a pizza joint and made absolute pigs of themselves. Amber thoroughly enjoyed that, too.

"Wow, I don't think I can walk," Mark said as they made their way to his car.

"You don't have to walk, you have to drive," Harriet retorted.

They climbed into his car. Amber and Brandon got into the backseat. Mark turned to them. "Uh, I think I'll drop you two off first. I, uh, want to borrow a book from Harriet and I don't want you to have to wait in the car."

"That's fine." Amber yawned. "I'm tired enough to crash out."

"Drop me first," Brandon said. "I live about a mile beyond Amber. That way you won't have to double back."

They dropped Brandon off and got to the mobile home park in less than ten minutes. Mark slowed down as he approached the entrance gate. "Which way do I turn when I get inside?"

"Just drop me off here," she said. "It's kind of a maze in there unless you know your way around."

"Are you sure?" He stopped the car. "I don't mind driving in."

"It's not worth the hassle," she replied as she opened the car door. "Unless you know exactly where to go, you'd end up having to back most of the way out. I'll be fine, really. This is pretty safe territory."

"Okay, if you're sure." To Mark's credit, he didn't look happy about dumping her.

Amber climbed out and shut the car door. "Thanks for taking me. I had a great evening. I'll call you tomorrow," she said to Harriet, "and you can give me directions to your house."

"I'll give you a lift if you need one," Mark promised.

They said good night and then Amber hurried into the park. She'd reached the first corner when she heard loud, fast footsteps behind her. She turned and looked.

There was someone standing by the entrance. Someone tall.

Amber stared for a moment, trying to make out the face.

But she was too far away. There was something menacing about the way the person just stood there, staring at her.

She took a deep breath and started walking up the street.

Nervous now, she glanced over her shoulder. The figure had started walking, too. Only now she could see it was a he. And he was walking fast.

Very fast.

Amber increased her pace and tried to pull her

house keys out of her purse as she walked. She turned the corner and started to run.

From behind her, she could hear that he'd begun to run, too.

But she knew something he didn't know. A shortcut. She flew through a dark passageway between two mobile homes, ducked behind a utility shed and emerged beside Lucy's mobile home.

Amber's spirits soared as she saw there were lights on at her place. She flew past Lucy's and pounded on her own front door.

"Celia!" she called. "Celia, please. Open up. It's me, Amber."

The front door flew open. "What the hell's going on? You're pounding loud enough to wake the dead."

Amber pointed toward the main entrance. "Someone's following me."

"Following you?"

"I think it's Jack Redden."

Chapter
Six

Dear Diary,
I don't know whether to be mad or to feel stupid. Celia
and Dale went charging out to try to catch the guy who
was following me and there wasn't anyone there. Dale
even got in his car and drove around. But he didn't see
or hear anyone. Nada, zip, zilch. No footsteps in the
dark, no headlights from a mysterious car. Nothing.
When they came in, they looked at me like I was mak-
ing the whole thing up.

I couldn't believe it. Why would they think I'd make
something like this up? Who would be dumb enough to
do something like that? Apparently they think I would.
I don't know what to do now. I know it was Jack Red-
den out there. But why? Why is he doing this to me?

Okay, so I didn't let him copy my stupid quiz paper.
Get real, that's hardly the crime of the century. It's not

*like I told everyone he was a pervert or slit the tires on
his fancy car. I just don't understand it.*

    Amber tossed her diary to one side and stared up at
the ceiling. From the living room, she could still hear
Dale and Celia talking in low voices. She was fairly
sure they were talking about her. About what a paranoid loony toon she'd become.

    "I'm not paranoid," she muttered. She put her diary
away and climbed between the sheets. "I'm not."

    But it was a long time before she fell asleep.

    Celia was gone the next morning when Amber
woke up. There was a note on the television saying she
and Dale were going to Palm Springs for the weekend.
Amber sighed. Great, another weekend spent alone.
Celia wasn't the greatest company in the world, but
she was better than nothing.

    Then Amber remembered she was going to Har-
riet's and that cheered her enormously. Maybe her
weekend wouldn't be so bad, she decided as she went
into the kitchen. Hungry, she headed for the fridge.

    It won't be too lonely, she told herself. She'd stay
busy. Yeah . . . She'd opened the door and got a carton
of orange juice. That's what she'd do. She'd clean the
house and do her laundry. Then she'd start her homework. And maybe, if there was time before Mark
picked her up, she'd take a quick swim. It wouldn't be
too bad. She poured the juice and reached over and
turned on the radio. Classic rock poured into the
kitchen. Amber started singing along with the Eagles
as she unloaded the dishwasher.

    Cleaning the house was easy, both she and Celia

were pretty neat so there wasn't much picking up to do. Amber had just finished scrubbing out the bathtub when the phone rang. She wiped her hands off and went to answer it. As she reached for the receiver, she remembered the menacing figure who'd stalked her last night. "Hello," she said warily.

"Hi, it's Chris."

Relief shot through her. "Hi."

"You busy today?" he asked.

"Just doing some housework," she replied. She decided the homework could wait until Sunday. "Why?"

"You want to go for a swim and then catch a movie?"

"I'd love to." She hesitated. "Uh, but instead of a movie, a friend of mine is having a few people over to her house. Would you like to go?"

"That sounds good," he said. "I've got some stuff to take care of and then I'll be by. How about we hit the pool around four-thirty? Then I can spend an hour or so with my grandmother before we go out tonight. Is that cool?"

"Sounds good to me."

They hung up and Amber flew into action. She charged into her bedroom and pulled her pale pink tank top and white slacks out of the pile of dirty clothes. She went to the small laundry room off the kitchen and tossed the clothes in the washer. Then she rushed to the phone, picked it up and dialed. Harriet answered after two rings. "Hello."

"Hi, Harriet, it's me, Amber."

"Oh, hi, I hope you're not calling to say you can't come tonight."

"No way." Amber cleared her throat. "But I was calling about tonight. Uh, do you mind if I bring some-one? Remember that guy I told you about?"

"Chris Bartlett. I told you I know who he is," Harriet said. "He went to Lansdale High. He was a BMOC."

Amber frowned. "What's that?"

"Jeez, you have been living in a cave. It's Big Man on Campus." Harriet laughed. "You're bringing him? Wow! That's cool."

"He asked me to go to the movies with him, but I told him I already had plans," Amber admitted. "Uh, I hope you don't mind that I invited him without ask-ing."

"Of course not," Harriet said. "Bring him along. Come by around seven. I've invited a couple of other kids so it should be fun."

"Anyone I know?"

"No." Harriet hesitated. "Actually, they're kids I met on-line. Oh, okay, I might as well confess. Two of them are driving over from Santa Barbara and I haven't even met them in person. They may be real geeks. That's one of the reasons I'm so glad you and Mark are going to be there."

Amber thought about that. "Don't worry," she fi-nally said. "I'll bet they're nice. If you like them on-line, there's no reason you wouldn't like them in person."

"Maybe they'll be worse than geeks." Harriet sounded really depressed now. "Maybe they'll be se-rial killers or something. Oh, God, what have I done? My parents would have a cow if they knew I'd invited people from the Internet. If they knew I'd given out my address and phone number to perfect strangers. Oh, God . . ."

"Harriet," Amber interrupted, "get a grip. They're not serial killers. They're probably perfectly normal people who are just as scared as you are. You met them in a teen chat room, right?"

"Yes, but so what? Any freak can go on-line and pretend to be seventeen."

"They can try," Amber argued. "But don't you think you'd be able to tell if they were faking it?"

"How? I'm a geek myself," Harriet cried. "Anyone could fool me. Oh, God, why didn't I keep my mouth shut? Why did I have to invite them?"

"Get a grip," Amber repeated. "You won't be alone tonight. You'll have friends with you. If they turn out to be freaky, we'll find a way to get them to leave."

"But they'll have my address—they'll know where I live."

"So do lots of other people," Amber pointed out, "and most of them don't come looking for you with a hatchet. Come on, lighten up. Tonight's going to be fun."

"I hope so," Harriet said. "I've never had many friends before. My parents are always cramming school down my throat. It's always grades, grades, grades. The only reason they're lightening up now is because I threatened not to go to college if they didn't let me have some fun. For crying out loud, it's my senior year and this is the first time I've ever had kids over to my house. I really want us to have a fun evening."

"We will," Amber promised. "Trust me on this. We'll have a great time tonight."

Chris and Amber spent over an hour in the pool and then he went to his grandmother's while Amber got ready for the evening. He picked her up at a quarter to seven and they drove up to Harriet's house in the local foothills.

She lived in one of the most exclusive housing tracts in the county. The large, Spanish-style house stood at the end of a cul-de-sac. It overlooked a deep, rocky arroyo.

"Wow," Amber said as she got out of the car, "I'll bet the view from up here is fabulous."

"It is," Chris agreed. He flashed her a grin. "I live a couple of blocks from here. From up here you can see all the way to Santa Barbara."

"So that's how you knew how to get here," Amber laughed. She wasn't intimidated by Harriet's big house or even by knowing that Chris lived in the same tract. She might live in a mobile home park, but she wasn't a pauper. Not by a long shot.

They walked up the red tile walkway, through a gate and across a beautiful enclosed courtyard to the front door. Chris reached for the doorbell, but before he could ring it the door flew open.

"Hi, I heard you coming." Harriet smiled shyly. She had on a pale yellow tank top, a short black skirt and strappy black sandals. Her hair was done, she was wearing her contacts and she'd put on just enough makeup to highlight her delicate features.

"This is Chris Bartlett," Amber introduced her date.

"I'm Harriet Islington." She extended her hand and they shook.

"We had a chemistry class together last year," Chris said. "You sat a couple of rows in front of me."

"Oh my gosh, you remember. Wasn't Mr. Corrigan the worst?" Harriet laughed and opened the door wider. "Come on in, Mark's already here and stuffing his face with guacamole and chips."

"Hey, I heard that." Mark came out into the foyer, holding a handful of chips. "It's not as if there's a chip shortage," he quipped. "I don't know how many people you're expecting tonight, but there's enough in there to feed the entire cast and crew of *Road Rules*. Hi." He extended the hand without the chips toward Chris. "I'm Mark."

"Chris Bartlett." They shook.

"I know who you are. You play one mean game of football."

"Not anymore," Chris said. "My knees took one hit too many. But thanks all the same."

"Let's go into the living room." Harriet led the way across the tiled foyer, down a short set of stairs to the living room.

Amber tried not to gape, but it was impossible. The far side of the room had huge plate-glass windows revealing a view of the arroyo and the surrounding hills that was spectacular.

The carpet was the color of new bricks and thick enough to sleep on and there was a fireplace big enough to roast an ox. Colorful paintings of African-Americans were hanging on the pale rose-colored walls and even Amber's untrained eye could tell the artworks were originals, not prints.

There was a rectangular oak coffee table covered with food in front of the hearth and matching end tables next to the love seats and couch.

"Have a seat," Harriet invited, "and I'll put on some music." She went to the CD player, which was housed behind the smoke-colored glass of an oak entertainment center near the entry door. "What do you all like? I've got rock, reggae and blues."

"You have any Bob Marley?" Chris asked as he and Amber made their way to the couch.

"You like reggae?" Mark asked. He plopped down in the love seat, reached over and scooped up another handful of chips.

"It's the best," Chris replied. He sighed in appreciation as the sweet, mellow sound of Marley filled the air.

Harriet joined them. "What would you like to drink?" she asked, smiling at Chris and Amber.

"I'll have a Coke," Chris replied.

"Me, too," Amber agreed.

"Be back in a sec." Harriet started to leave.

"I'll come with you," Amber said. "I want to see your kitchen."

"He's really nice," Harriet whispered as soon as they were out of earshot. "Not stuck up at all."

"He's cool." Amber came to a complete stop. The kitchen was unbelievable. Copper pots and pans hung artfully over a large, center island. There was a double-sized stainless steel fridge, two sinks, a stove with six burners and miles of counter space.

"My mom likes to cook," Harriet admitted. She seemed a bit embarrassed so Amber restrained herself from gushing. But the place was incredible.

"I'll bet she's good at it, too," Amber replied.

"Actually," Harriet said as she opened the fridge and pulled out a six-pack of Coke, "She is. They host a lot of dinner parties for my dad's business associates. She made the guacamole and the other dips. Be sure to try them."

"I will." She laughed. "If there's any left by the time we get back in there. Mark was making a real dent in the food and let me warn you, Chris is no amateur when it comes to eating, too."

Harriet laughed, but the sound seemed forced. She busied herself getting ice and pouring the Cokes.

"Harriet," Amber said softly, "stop worrying. If your friends aren't nice, we'll get them to leave."

"I'm not exactly worried," she denied. She put the drinks on a tray. "Well, okay, I am. I don't know what got into me. It's not like me to do something so dumb. What am I gonna say when these strangers show up? I don't know them."

"It wasn't dumb and you do know them," Amber insisted. She put her arm around Harriet's shoulders. "And if there's any problem, you've got me and Chris and Mark here. We're your friends, we won't let you down."

"Thanks." Harriet smiled. "That means a lot."

The doorbell rang. Harriet almost jumped out of her skin. "Oh, God, that's them."

Amber scooped up the tray with the drinks. "Get Mark to go to the door with you. I'll take these in."

"Okay." Harriet, with one last worried look at Amber, headed back to the living room.

Amber followed more slowly. She didn't want to risk dumping Coke on the plush carpet. She set the tray down in front of Chris.

"Is there a problem?" he asked softly. He cut a quick look toward the foyer.

Amber hadn't told him about Harriet's fears. She hadn't wanted to embarrass her friend by telling tales. "Not really, it's just that Harriet's never met these friends in the flesh. They're chat room buddies and she's a little nervous."

"I see." Chris got to his feet as Harriet and Mark came back. Two people came in behind them. One was a short, blond boy wearing a blue-and-black striped shirt, baggy black pants and a ring through his nose. The other was a thin, henna-haired girl dressed in a gray tank top and jeans.

"These are my friends," Harriet said, "Amber, Mark and Chris." She turned her head and smiled at the newcomers, "And this is Tracy Rickman"—she pointed at the girl—"and Jason Wills."

"Hi." Tracy stuck her head out from behind Harriet. "Nice to meet you."

"Hi." Jason waggled his fingers in a wave.

"Uh, have a seat. What would you like to drink?" Harriet asked.

"Coke," they both answered at once. They moved awkwardly toward the love seat and plopped down. It was obvious to Amber that Tracy and Jason were just as nervous as Harriet.

"I'll get it." Harriet fled toward the kitchen. "Make yourselves at home."

No one spoke for a moment. Chris reached over and snagged some chips. He dunked one in the dip. "Have some guacamole," he invited. "It's really good. Where do you two go to school?"

"West Valley High," Jason answered. "We're both seniors."

"You planning on going to college after you graduate?" Mark asked. He reached past the dip and snagged a piece of cheese off the tray.

"Yeah." Jason glanced nervously toward the kitchen. "Uh, I'm trying to get into film school somewhere . . ."

"Hey, cool," Mark said enthusiastically. "Me, too. Had any luck yet?"

Jason visible relaxed. "Not yet. I've been accepted into a couple of places but I'm waiting to see if I make USC or UCLA."

"Me, too." Mark shook his head. "I don't care which one lets me in, I just want one of them to come through."

"You got a backup position?" Jason asked. "Someplace to go if neither of the biggies comes through?"

Mark shrugged. "If that happens, I'll go to the local JC and then transfer."

"That's the easiest way to get in," Tracy said softly. She popped open her purse, which was on the love seat next to her, and took out a tissue. "That's how my brother did it. He goes to UCLA."

"Is he in the film school?" Mark shoved more chips in his mouth.

She nodded. "He really likes it, too."

"Are you interested in film?" Amber asked Tracy.

Tracy shook her head. "I want to study literature. I like to write. That's one of the reasons I wanted to meet Harriet. She's been so supportive of my writing. Always encouraging me, always telling me I can do it . . ."

"Harriet's the best," Mark interjected. He broke off, grinning with embarrassment as he realized she'd come back into the room.

Harriet sat a small tray of soft drinks in tall, frosty glasses on the table and handed one to Tracy.

"Thanks." Tracy took the drink.

She finished playing hostess and sat down next to Mark. She'd relaxed in the last few minutes. "Please go on," she told him. "I believe you were just getting to the part about me being 'the best.'"

Mark groaned dramatically. "I refuse to say another word. I don't want to be responsible for your head getting so big you can't get through the door."

Everyone laughed and the tension in the room eased. The conversation began to flow easily and naturally. Soon they were talking about movies and books and life.

Mark took charge of the CD player and kept a steady stream of good music playing in the background. Harriet, Amber and Tracy brought the rest of the food from the kitchen and everyone stuffed themselves silly.

"Is there any more Coke left?" Mark held up his empty glass. "I'm parched."

"Give your tongue a rest," Harriet suggested, "maybe that'll help."

"Very funny"—he made a face at her—"coming from someone who talks so much she makes me look tongue-tied."

"I'm thirsty, too," Chris put in.

"I'll bring out more soda." Harriet stood up. "If you want a refill, put your glass on the tray." She looked pointedly at Amber. "Uh, I could use some help."

Amber, who'd been deeply involved in a conversation with Chris about restaurants that neither of them had ever been to, jumped to her feet. "I can take a hint."

They went into the kitchen. As soon as they were out of earshot, Harriet shook her head. "I can't believe I was such a jerk about Jason and Tracy. They're really, really nice. I'm so glad I invited them."

"They are nice," Amber agreed. "And interesting, too. Chris and I are going to go see a couple of the flicks that Jason's talked about."

"You two becoming an item?" Harriet set the tray of multi-colored glasses on the center island.

Amber sighed. "I don't know."

"Don't know? What does that mean?" Harriet pulled a couple more of the big bottles of soda out of the fridge and put them next to the tray.

Amber bit her lip. This was so hard to admit. "It means I've never had a boyfriend before. I've never really dated. I know that makes me sound like some kind of pathetic dork . . ."

"If you're a dork then I'm a geek," Harriet interrupted. She unscrewed the top of one of the soda bottles. "At least you've got an excuse for never dating. You were taking care of your mom, right? What about me? I've never dated either and the only excuse I have is that I'm a nerd."

"You're not a nerd," Amber insisted. "You're smart and you're pretty and any guy would love to go out with you. Look at Mark, he's been drooling over you all evening."

"Really?" Harriet brightened immediately. "You're not just saying that?"

"No, I'm not just saying it," Amber grinned broadly. "I think he really likes you."

"I hope so." Harriet sighed dreamily. "I really like him, too. But, God, it's so hard to know how to get from being just his friend to being . . . well, you know, something more."

"Don't look at me for any answers. I've never even had a date. Uh, would your parents have a problem with you going out with Mark?"

"Yeah." She sighed again, only this time it wasn't dreamy. "But not because he's white and we're not."

"Then why?" Amber picked up a bottle and began to pour.

"They don't want anything distracting me from my studies." She made a face. "I told you, I had to threaten them just to let me go out last night and have this get-together. They're fanatical about my studies. Going to a good school is the Holy Grail for my folks. Oh, don't get me wrong. They want me to be happy, but they'd rather I was smart than popular. It took me three years to talk them into letting me wear contacts. They were afraid the contacts would make me, uh . . ."

"Pretty and popular." Amber laughed. "Well, they were right. They have. Just look, you're here with a houseful of your friends and you've got a guy practically tripping over his tongue whenever he sees you."

Harriet laughed. "That's me. Social butterfly. I'll bet I'm the only butterfly in the forest that's never even had a date."

"There's me. It's reassuring to know I'm not the only social misfit around."

"We're not social misfits," Harriet said. "We're late bloomers." She finished filling up the glasses and lifted hers off the tray. "Let's have a toast."

Amber got her glass and raised it. "To late bloomers."

The girls clinked glasses and then burst out laughing. Just then, Mark stuck his head in. "Hey, what's the holdup here? We're dying of thirst."

"Keep your shirt on," Amber called. "We'll be there in a minute."

Harriet carried the heavy tray and Amber got the door. Chris smiled at Amber as she sat down next to him. "Everything okay?"

She nodded. "Everything's fine. We're just slow."

Harriet set the tray down and served the sodas. "Wasn't it clever of me to use different colored glasses for all of us? At least we're spared each other's cooties."

Everyone howled.

"Cooties! Jeez, I haven't heard that one since third grade." Mark laughed.

Harriet giggled. "I know. But it was always one of my favorite insults." She handed a Coke to Tracy.

"Mine, too. Thanks," Tracy said as she took the drink. "Oh darn, it's dripping a little. Here, I can fix that . . ." Holding the glass in one hand, she reached for a napkin. As she leaned forward, her hip brushed against her open purse and toppled it forward. Something rolled out onto the floor and under the coffee table.

"Oh darn. Sorry about that." Tracy handed the Coke to Jason and bent down. She peeked under the table.

"Is this what you're looking for?" Amber picked up the brightly colored can. It had stopped next to her toe. She frowned as she read the label. "Pepper spray?"

Tracy gave an embarrassed shrug. "My mom makes me carry it. She was mugged last summer. It was broad daylight, too. Scared the crap out of her. So she went out and bought a truckload of this stuff." She laughed nervously. "She makes everyone in the family carry it."

"Can I see it?" Mark asked eagerly.

"It's just an aerosol can," Harriet chided. She'd plopped down next to Mark and, despite her words, she was staring curiously at the cannister in Amber's hand.

"Does it work?" Amber asked. She squinted, trying to read the small print on the back of the can.

"I don't know," Tracy admitted. "I've never had to use it."

"My mom has," Jason interjected. "She used it on some punk that tried to snatch her purse."

"What happened?" Harriet asked.

"Some kid ran at her and tried to make a fast grab

for her purse." Jason handed Tracy her Coke. "Mom saw him coming, though. So he didn't get it."

"If he grabbed at her purse, how'd she get the spray out?" Chris asked. "Don't women carry everything in their purses?"

"She had it in her coat pocket. She got it out in time to blast him one right in the face."

"What happened to him?" Harriet asked softly. "I mean, is it like tear gas? Does it hurt? Does it do permanent damage? Was he hospitalized?"

"Nah," Jason replied. "He was okay. It's just pepper and water. When it hit his eyes it hurt some. But it was enough to make him back off and more important it gave my mom time to get away."

"Good." Harriet stood up again. "Oh my gosh, I didn't realize it was so late. I hate to be a party pooper but in about ten minutes my parents are going to be home. You're welcome to stay and meet them. They're nice, but nosy."

Everyone laughed.

Chris looked questioningly at Amber and she nodded. He stood up. "We'll get going, if it's all the same to you." He leaned down and picked up paper plates and dirty napkins. "I've had enough nosy parents for one day."

Everyone else stood and started clearing up.

Amber handed the can back to Tracy. "Where did your mom get this stuff?"

Tracy thought for a moment. "I'm not sure. Uh, but I can find out if you want me to."

"I do."

"I'll ask my mom. Give me a call," Tracy said. "Harriet's got my number."

Amber nodded her thanks and began to help with the cleanup.

A few minutes later, they'd said their good-byes and were on their way. Amber waved at Tracy and Jason as they pulled away from the curb.

"Amber," Chris said softly as they walked to his car. "I hope you're not thinking of getting that stuff."

"Why not?" She waited while he unlocked the car door. "I'm alone a lot. Celia's gone more often than she's home."

He shrugged. "I guess that stuff just makes me nervous. My grandma wanted some, so I did some research on it." He walked around and got in the driver's side. "There's a lot of evidence that when women try to use this stuff, their attacker takes it away from them. It just gives the attacker one more weapon."

"I see," she murmured.

"Besides," he said as he put the key in the ignition, "what do you need it for? This isn't L.A., it's Lansdale. What could possibly happen to you here?"

Chapter
Seven

Dear Diary,
I had a fabulous time tonight. It was so much fun
hanging out with my friends. Celia's gone so much, I
wonder if she'd mind if I had them over some weekend? I'd have to buy some more CDs and the food and
stuff, but that's not a problem. I'll ask her when she
gets home tomorrow night, that is, if she comes home.

Chris is so cool. He came in when he brought me
home and we talked for another hour. He's not just
good-looking, he's also easy to talk to—he's one of
those people who are really, really good listeners. My
mom was like that. Before you know it you spill your
guts about everything. I was tempted to tell him about
my problem with Redden. Okay, I'll admit it, the creep
has me a little rattled. After all, I am alone here for the
weekend. Anyway, I was really tempted to say something, but I chickened out at the last minute. To be hon-

*est I didn't want Chris thinking I was some kind of
loser that all the other kids in school picked on.*

Amber stared at the words she'd just written and
sighed. She glanced at the phone lying on the bedside
table and bit her lip. She wished Chris would call. She
wished she'd had the courage to tell him about what
was going on. But she couldn't handle it if he thought
there was something wrong with her. Like she was a
loser or something. Would he think that? And if he did,
what did that say about him? She shook her head in
disgust. This was getting her nowhere! She wasn't
going to say anything to him. She couldn't take the
risk. She didn't want Chris to know. Period.

She closed her diary and tossed it into the bedside
drawer. She was tired and there was no point in worrying
about what Chris would think. He'd either understand or
he wouldn't. And as for Jack, the door was locked and
she was a light sleeper. If she heard anything, if she
heard so much as a bump or a scrape or a creak, she'd
punch the speed dial for 911 and the cops would be here
in minutes. She'd scream her head off, too.

Amber spent Sunday finishing her homework, doing a
few chores that didn't really need doing and watching
TV. She tried calling Harriet and Chris, but neither of
them were at home. The only scary thing that happened was another phone call. But this time, Amber
kept her cool. She could hear him breathing on the
other end. She knew who it was, of course. But instead
of saying anything, instead of reacting at all, she simply stayed on the line.

After a few minutes, he hung up.

Amber unplugged the phone. It had taken every ounce of nerve she had to remain silent, to not scream her lungs out at Redden. She didn't like the thought of missing a call from Chris or Harriet or even Celia, but she'd take the risk rather than give Redden another shot at her.

Amber plugged the phone back in when she heard Celia's Toyota pull up outside late that night.

"How was it around here?" Celia asked. She popped her overnight bag next to the couch and kicked off her shoes. "Any problems?"

"Only a creepy phone call," Amber replied.

Celia raised an eyebrow, "Creepy how?"

"You know, it rang, I answered it and there was no one there. Only there was someone there because I could hear them breathing."

"Maybe it was just a wrong number?"

Amber shook her head. "They stayed on the line too long for that."

"When did it happen?" Celia stifled a yawn.

"Today."

Celia stared at her for a long moment. "You don't look traumatized by the incident. Weren't you scared?"

"I would have been it I hadn't been half-expecting it," Amber answered honestly. "But Jack's not very smart. He tends to repeat himself and he's done the phone thing before."

"I'm glad to see you're taking it in stride." Celia yawned. "What'd you do this weekend?"

"I went to a friend's house for a get-together. Chris Bartlett took me."

"Lucy Bartlett's grandson?"

"That's right. We went to Harriet's house. When he brought me home, he came in for a while. You don't mind, do you?" Amber thought it was a little late for Celia to try playing the heavy-handed guardian routine, but she owed the woman the courtesy of the truth.

Celia hesitated. "Uh, I guess not. You're a good kid. You don't do drugs or drink, do you?"

Amber managed to keep a straight face. Barely. "Do you think I'd admit it if I did? But for the record, no. I don't do booze or drugs."

"Okay then." Celia started toward the kitchen. "It's fine if you want to have your friends over. Just let me know in advance, okay?"

"Of course. Uh, what are we going to do about the phone call?"

"Nothing," Celia called over her shoulder. "The only thing we can do is have the number changed. Unless you want to file a police report or something."

"I don't want to do that unless I have to," Amber said. She followed her cousin into the kitchen and leaned against the counter. "Maybe he'll get bored and leave me alone."

"You don't know that it was that Redden kid." Celia opened the fridge and took out a soda. "Maybe it was just a crank call. They do happen, you know."

"Maybe," Amber agreed. But she knew it hadn't been a crank call. It had been Jack Redden and she knew darned good and well he wasn't going to leave her alone. As a matter of fact, she had a feeling he was going to get even nastier.

For once, Amber hoped she'd be wrong.

•   •   •

On the way to school the next morning, she pumped Brandon for any additional information he knew about Jack. But Brandon didn't seem to want to talk about it.

When it was time to go to history, she stood outside the classroom for a moment and took a long, deep breath. She wouldn't be bullied. She wouldn't. From the corner of her eye, she saw Julie Steadman coming up the walkway toward the classroom. Amber turned and stared.

Julie's eyes widened for a split second. Amber started toward her. She wasn't sure what she was going to say, but she was going to say something. Julie came to a dead stop, a look of panic on her pretty face. Her mouth gaped open in shock as Amber advanced toward her. Suddenly, she whirled around and took off running.

Stunned, Amber watched her charge toward the student parking lot.

"What was that all about?" Harriet said as she came to stand next to Amber. She was looking down the walkway as were dozens of other kids.

"I think she's afraid of me," Amber replied.

"Was she scared you were going to kick her butt or something?" Harriet asked incredulously.

"I guess so." Amber shook her head. "But all I wanted to do was talk to her, ask her why she did it."

"We know why," Harriet insisted. "She did it to get back at you for changing seats with John Berry. She's got a huge crush on him. Either that, or Jack Redden paid her to do it."

Amber stared at Harriet in disbelief. "Paid her to do it? You've got to be kidding."

"Wish I was." Harriet shrugged and jerked her chin toward the classroom door. "Come on, let's go. I don't want to be late."

Amber kept thinking of Julie. Why had she run? Surely the girl wasn't scared that Amber would take a swing at her. But maybe she was. Maybe underneath all that blonde coolness, Julie Steadman was a big old-fashioned coward.

As she went to her seat, she saw that Jack was already there. She stared him straight in the eyes. He smirked at her. Sneered, actually. Amber narrowed her gaze and swung into her own seat. She put on a good show, but inside she was shaking.

During class, she tried to listen to Mr. Powers, but it was hard. She could feel Jack's eyes boring a hole in her back. The bell finally rang. Her first instinct was to make a run for it, to get the heck out of there as fast as she could. But she'd done that before and it hadn't helped. He was still harassing her. So she made herself move at a leisurely pace. She picked up her backpack and slung it over her shoulder and then joined the other kids pouring out of the front door.

Outside, she looked around to see if Harriet had waited for her, but Amber didn't see her. Harriet usually took off out the back door and headed for her locker on the other side of campus to get her lunch.

Amber started toward the library. She knew he was right behind her—she could feel him.

"Ouch!" she yelped as the back of her heel was raked by a foot. Amber whirled around.

"Oh, I'm sorry, Did I accidentally step on your dainty little foot?" Jack gave her an evil grin. Billy Palato was right beside him. He sneered at Amber.

"It wasn't an accident," she challenged.

"But it was," Jack insisted in a high-pitched singsong voice. "Just ask Billy. He saw the whole thing."

"Yeah, it was an accident." Billy bobbed his head up and down. "But then, you're kinda accident-prone, aren't you? Heard you almost got hit by a car the other day. That's pretty stupid. God, even my dog's not that dumb. . . . Hey, why'd you do that?" Billy jumped as Jack elbowed him sharply in the gut.

"You're not getting away with this," Amber said. She forced herself to face him even though she felt like running as fast as she could. "I'm not going to be bullied."

Several kids had stopped and were openly watching them. Others, either because they were scared of Jack or because they were hungry for lunch, charged past them without so much as a second glance.

He leaned toward her until he was only inches from her face. She stood her ground. "You're not going to be bullied," he echoed. "Get this straight, bitch: I don't let anyone push me around."

"I wasn't pushing you around. You're the one bothering me."

Jack kept on talking like he didn't even hear her. "I get even. I always get even. You should have thought of that before you went running to the vice principal. I get even."

Amber swallowed but didn't lower her eyes. She knew that more kids had stopped to watch them and that having an audience would only make him even worse, but she knew she couldn't let him see how scared she was. She said nothing—she simply looked him dead in the eyes. She was determined to stare Redden down, even if she had to stand there all day.

"Hey, Amber." Brandon Yates's voice cut through the now-silent area. "Come on, it's lunchtime. We're waiting for you."

"You'd better go running to your friends, bitch." Redden's lips curled in an ugly sneer. "Enjoy them now. By the time I'm through with you, you won't have any left."

"I think I will," she said. Then she turned on her heel and walked toward Brandon. He was standing at the corner of the building. He tried to look casual, but she could see the worry in his eyes. She gave him a strained smile as he fell into step with her. "Thanks for the rescue."

"Jeez." Brandon shook his head in disbelief. "Why were you having a face-off with that jerk?"

"He's been harassing me," she said quietly. "And I'm sick of it."

"He's an asshole," Brandon agreed. "But watch your back. According to some people, he's a dangerous one."

"If he's so dangerous why is he still here?" Amber asked. "He should have been expelled for what he's done to me. But all the school's done is call him into the office and slap him on the wrist."

"I think we both know the answer to that," Brandon muttered.

"You got that right," Amber agreed. But she wondered what she was going to do. Redden wasn't scared of the vice principal. He knew that they wouldn't do a darned thing to a student whose parents gave fifty thousand dollars to the school athletic program.

At lunch, Amber pushed her problems to the back of her mind. At least she tried to, but it was hard. Harriet and Mark were now openly mooning over each other and Brandon had to leave after a few minutes to go to the library.

The bell rang and Amber grabbed her stuff. "Come on, Harriet, we'll be late if you don't move it."

Harriet gave Mark a dreamy smile. "See ya."

"I'll call you tonight." Mark's smile was equally goofy. "About eight, okay?"

"Okay."

"Come on, Harriet," Amber persisted. "We don't want to be late. Mrs. Martin can be a real pain if we're late." Their English teacher was as old as the hills and didn't cut anyone any slack.

With one last smile, Harriet picked up her backpack, waved at Mark and fell into step with Amber. They crossed the quad to the main building. "Isn't he wonderful?" Harriet murmured. "He's so sweet, so nice. He's perfect."

Amber rolled her eyes. "Yeah, he's great. Uh, look, Harriet, can I have Tracy's phone number?"

"Tracy who?"

"Tracy the girl we met at your house on Saturday night."

"Sure. I don't have it with me. I'll have to call you when I get home. Do you mind if I ask why you want it?"

Amber wasn't sure she was ready to admit the truth.

It would sound too weird. "Uh, she mentioned a restaurant down in L.A. that sounded really good. But I can't remember the name." The girls reached the big double doors leading to the main building. Amber pulled them open. "It sounded like a good place. I, uh, thought maybe Chris and I would give it a try sometime."

Harriet nodded absently. "Isn't it great having a boyfriend?"

Amber didn't really think one date meant that Chris was her boyfriend, but she didn't want to argue the point. "Yeah, sure. You know, Jack Redden tried to run me down after history class. How come you took off so fast? It would have been nice to have a witness. You know, someone who could say I wasn't nuts."

"I have to go clear across campus to my locker to get my lunch, you know that."

"I know, but you could have waited for me. I'd have gone with you." They reached the stairs leading to the second floor.

"I'm sorry." Harriet shrugged. "I didn't know you needed a baby-sitter."

"Baby-sitter? I hardly think wanting someone to witness what that jerk is doing means I want a baby-sitter," Amber replied. She tried not to be hurt by her friend's callous attitude.

"Oh jeez, I didn't mean that the way it sounded," Harriet apologized. "If I'd known Jack was going to get up to his old tricks, I'd have waited for you. The truth is, I thought he'd backed off some since your cousin called the school and complained."

"It's okay, I understand. I shouldn't have said anything. You're right—I can't expect other people to baby-sit me just because of that pig."

"No, you're right," Harriet insisted. "We're friends and I should have waited. I knew the bastard was giving you a bad time. The real truth is, I was in such a hurry to see Mark, I completely forgot about your problems. I'm sorry."

They'd reached their classroom so she and Harriet didn't get a chance to finish their conversation.

The afternoon passed quickly. When the last bell rang, Amber hurried to her locker. She was relieved to see that there was no more writing on it. She reached up, dialed the combination and pulled the door open.

A flood of water poured down on her. "What the—" She leapt back as a small plastic bucket that had been propped up on a stack of books fell out and bounced on the concrete.

Other students, attracted by her yell and the noise of the water slapping against the concrete, stared at her as they walked past. The two kids at the lockers a few feet down from hers laughed.

Her cheeks flamed with humiliation. Embarrassed, she tried to ignore the giggles that seemed to come from all around her. They wouldn't think it was so darned funny if it had happened to any of them.

"Jeez, Amber, what happened?" Brandon cut through the crowd and rushed over to her.

Amber wiped her cheeks and kicked the bucket as hard as she could. "Someone propped a full bucket of water in my locker. When I opened it, I got it right in the face."

He whistled through his teeth. "Man, that's a tough

trick to pull off." He opened the locker and looked inside. "They must have propped the bucket with this stick." He leaned down and picked up a stick that was right beneath the locker. She hadn't noticed it falling out. "See," Brandon continued, "if you fill the bucket with water and prop it with a stick against the metal slats on the inside of the door, when you open it, the stick will fall away and the bucket tumbles out."

"How'd he get my combination?" she asked. She knew who'd done this.

The other kids had started moving off by now. Brandon shrugged. "He probably bullied someone in the attendance office into giving it to him. Your locker combination is written on the back of your emergency number card."

"I'm going to report this," she said. "I've had it." She turned and started for the administration building.

"Hey, wait up. I'll come with you." He slammed her locker shut, picked up the empty bucket and hurried after her.

Kids stared at them as they crossed the campus but Amber didn't care. She'd had it. If that stupid vice principal didn't do something about this, she'd blow a gasket. Yanking open the outer door, she stalked down the hall. The dragon lady, Mrs. Larchmont, looked up with a startled frown as Amber stormed into the office. Mr. Mullins's door was open. She could hear him talking on the phone.

"What happened to you?" Dragon Lady asked. She rose from her seat, her face more curious than concerned.

"Some jerk booby-trapped my locker."

"You mean someone played a joke on you." She smiled slightly.

"It wasn't very funny to me. I'd like to see Mr. Mullins, please."

"He's on the phone. You'll have to wait."

"I'll do that. By the way, how many people have access to my records?"

Dragon Lady shrugged. "I've no idea. In any case, that's not the sort of question I'm prepared to discuss with a student."

"That's okay," Amber retorted. "You can tell it to my lawyer."

"Lawyer?" Mr. Mullins stuck his head out. "Oh dear, what happened here?"

"Jack Redden booby-trapped my locker. When I opened it, this"—she grabbed the bucket out of Brandon's hand and held it up—"came flying into my face. I thought you said you were going to do something about him."

"Did you see Jack put the water in your locker?" Mr. Mullins asked.

"Who else would have done it?"

He shrugged and leaned casually against the door-jamb. "I don't know but I think it's unfair to blame Jack just because you and he have had a problem in the past."

"A problem?" Brandon interrupted. "Jeez, that bastard is trying to hurt her. Don't you people get it?"

"Young man, I don't believe this concerns you." Mr. Mullins straightened up and glared at Brandon.

Brandon stood his ground. "I'm a witness; doesn't that involve me?"

"Oh, for crying out loud, will you kids stop being so melodramatic?" Mr. Mullins sighed in disgust. "It was a dumb, stupid prank but it was hardly life-threatening."

"So you're not going to do anything about it?" Amber persisted. She wanted to make him admit it; she wanted to make him say it out loud.

Mr. Mullins raised his eyebrows. "And what, precisely, would you have me do?"

"I want you to drag Redden in here and tell him to leave me alone!" Amber cried. "I'm sick of having to watch my back every minute."

"How do you know it was Jack?" Mr. Mullins shook his head. "Unless you've got a witness, there's nothing we can do."

"You can investigate," she persisted. "You can find out who in this office gave Jack my locker combination. You can ask a few questions. I do have rights here. Hazing is illegal in this state."

Mullins's eyes narrowed and he dropped all pretense that this was a casual matter of little concern. He came over and stood on the other side of the counter, glaring at her. "No one here's been hazed. Some unknown person played a nasty trick on you, that's all . . ." Brandon snorted in disgust. Mr. Mullins shot him a dirty look as he continued. "And we'll do a thorough investigation, I assure you. However, I'm not going to be dragging someone in here for disciplinary action until I've got all the facts. Is that clear?"

"Yeah, it's clear all right," Amber replied. She handed Mr. Mullins the bucket. "Here, you'll need this." She turned and started for the door. Brandon, with one last disgusted look at Mullins, trailed after her.

"Thanks for trying to defend me in there," Amber said as soon as they were outside.

"Sorry it didn't do any good," he said. "You know that Mullins's investigation won't turn up squat, don't you? I'm not trying to depress you or anything, but I don't think you ought to get your hopes up either."

"How do you know so much about it?" Amber asked curiously.

Brandon shrugged. "Let's just say I've done this number before. A friend of mine was one of his victim's last year. This is like a rerun of a bad TV show. He went to the school administration, too. It didn't do Eric any good either. After he almost had a nervous breakdown, his folks pulled him out of here and he got his diploma at night school."

"That's not going to happen to me," Amber vowed. But even as she said the words they sounded hollow.

"Yeah, well, maybe you'll get lucky. Come on, let's get a move on. If we hurry, we might make the early bus."

When Celia came home from work that evening, Amber gave her a full report. But her cousin's attitude was just like the vice principal's. She didn't take it seriously. "You don't know that it was this Redden kid," she said. She headed down the hall.

Amber was right on her heels. "It has to be him. No one else hates me that much."

"I've got to change." Celia went into her bedroom and closed the door. "Dale and I are going bowling."

"Aren't you going to have dinner?" Amber asked through the door. "I've thawed out some ground beef. I was going to make hamburgers. I've got all the stuff." She didn't think she could face another meal alone.

"I don't have time. We're grabbing a bite at the bowling alley," Celia called out. "Dale's joined a league and we don't want to be late."

Amber sighed. Another solitary meal. Great. Maybe she'd fry up a burger and take it out to the pool. "Can you call the school tomorrow?"

"What about?"

What about? She couldn't believe her ears. "About Redden's horrible acts. First he tries to cripple me . . ."

"I thought you said he stepped on your heel?" Celia yelled through the closed bedroom door.

Amber ignored her. "And then he tried to brain me with a bucket of water."

The bedroom door opened and Celia, barefoot and wearing jeans and a T-shirt, stepped out. "I've already talked to the school. I'm sure they're doing everything they can. Have you seen my white sandals?"

Amber realized talking to her cousin was pointless. "They're under the coffee table."

"Thanks." Celia gave her a quick smile and darted down the hall. Depressed, Amber trudged after her.

Celia was standing next to the coffee table, slipping her feet into the sandals. "Don't look so glum, kid. I've put the school on notice. They know they'd better not let this boy keep bothering you."

"That didn't stop him today." Amber leaned against the overstuffed chair and stared at her cousin.

"Today's stuff was just a prank," Celia said. "Besides, you don't even know that he's the one who did it. Let's face it, you might just be the kind of kid that gets picked on. There was a girl like that at my high school." Celia looked around for her purse, spotted it lying on the other end of the couch and picked it up. "She was just one of those types, you know. People were always pulling stunts on the poor girl. But it was done as a joke, you know. It wasn't malicious."

"I'll bet she didn't find them funny." Amber knew what her cousin was implying. She was hinting that Amber was one of those pathetic types that the nice kids felt sorry for and the mean kids teased. Her spirits plummeted even lower.

Celia hurried toward the door. "Come on, lighten up. There was no harm done. See you later. Uh, don't wait up, I might be late."

"Now there's a surprise," Amber muttered as she watched the door close.

Depressed, Amber trudged into the kitchen. Opening the fridge, she pulled out the pound of hamburger and plopped it on the counter.

There was a knock on the front door.

"Who is it?" she called. She wasn't going to open the door until she knew darned good and well who was standing on the other side. It hadn't exactly been a great day and she was in no mood to fight off that lunatic Redden.

"It's me, Chris. Come on, open up. My hands are full."

Amber unlocked the door and flung it open. "Hi. What are you doing here?"

Chris, loaded down with half a dozen plastic grocery bags plunged inside. "Hi, I hope you don't mind my dropping by . . . I, uh, wondered if you wanted to have dinner with us. Can I set these down?"

"Let me help." She rushed over and took a bag of potatoes off him. "Just put them on the floor."

Chris dumped the bags and then sighed in relief. "Man, those are heavy. I picked up some groceries."

"For your grandma?"

"She doesn't like to shop," Chris explained.

"At her age, it's probably hard for her."

He snorted. "She never did like to grocery shop. Anyway, will you come have supper with us? Then I thought maybe we could go for a drive or something."

Amber glanced toward the counter. "I've already thawed out some ground beef . . . but I guess it'll keep until tomorrow. Sure, I'd love to come for supper."

He grinned and started picking up bags. "Cool. Grab your bathing suit and come on over."

"You want to go swimming?"

"Sure, why not? Grandma's going to make her famous meat loaf. That'll take at least an hour. She may hate to shop, but she loves to cook."

"Okay. You need any help with those bags?"

"Nah, I've got it. Come over when you're ready and we'll hit the pool."

"See you in a few minutes," she called as he left. Amber went to the kitchen and put the meat back in the refrigerator. Then she flew down the hall to her bedroom.

After she'd changed, she took a long, hard look at herself in the mirror. Amber made a face at her reflection. Her hair looked like it'd been whipped with an eggbeater. Drat, he'd seen her like this. She cringed. She turned and went to her backpack, which was lying on her bed. Unzipping the small pocket on the outside of the bag, she jammed her hand inside looking for her hairbrush. Amber yelped as something scurried across her hand. Heart racing, she leapt up as a small white mouse burst out of the bag and charged across the bed. The mouse plunged off the end of the bed, raced across the floor and out the door.

Amber calmed down. The poor mouse was even more scared than she was. "That was a lousy thing to do," she muttered in disgust. She wasn't really angry. When she was little, she'd had a whole series of mice, guinea pigs, and hamsters as pets.

Jack Redden had miscalculated when he'd pulled off this trick. She'd been startled, but not terrified. She wasn't scared of mice.

Amber stood up and took a long, steadying breath. In a few moments her heartbeat had slowed to normal. She looked at herself in the mirror. Her face was pale and her eyes wary. She didn't like this. Darn it, this was her senior year. She wanted to enjoy it, but how could she when she had to watch her back all the time?

It was obvious that neither the school nor Celia was going to be much help. Celia thought she was the kind of girl that got picked on and the school was too scared of Redden's rich parents to do anything useful.

She was on her own. She knew that now.

Jack Redden wasn't going to stop and she was tired of his stupid, sick games.

Maybe it was time to play a few of her own.

Chapter
Eight

"Everything okay?" Chris asked. They were standing in the shallow end of the pool after having swum for an hour.

Amber dipped back and plunged her hair in the water for a brief moment to get the heavy stuff out of her face. She thought about telling him everything, and then just before she opened her mouth, she remembered all the reasons she shouldn't. Celia's words came back to haunt her. *Maybe you're just one of those kids that gets picked on.* No, Amber decided, she would fight her own battles. There was no need to share her troubles with Chris. Not when they made her sound like a pathetic loser. "Things are fine," she lied. "Why do you ask?"

"No real reason." He shrugged. "You've just been kinda quiet. I wondered if maybe I'd done something to tick you off."

"Don't be silly." She forced a laugh. "Of course you haven't done something to tick me off. I've had a great time today. I'm just beat, that's all. Hey, shouldn't we get out and dry off? I distinctly remember Lucy telling us not to be late. I don't know about you, but I'm starved."

"You're changing the subject. But I'll let you off the hook as long as you promise nothing's wrong."

"Nothing's wrong," she insisted. She started for the edge of the pool. "Really."

"You're sure?" he pressed. He trudged up the pool steps, picked up their towels and tossed hers to her.

She wiped her face and then began to dry herself. She was flattered that he was so concerned, but she still wasn't going to open her mouth. "I'm sure. Gosh, I'd better get a move on. I'll meet you back at Lucy's."

Amber went back to her place to change. She put on a pair of pale pink shorts and a matching tank top. Grabbing her brush, she gave her hair a quick once-over, made a face at herself in the mirror and then hurried over to Lucy's. Chris opened the door when she knocked. "That was fast," he said. The aroma of homemade cooking came from the kitchen.

Her mouth watered as she stepped inside. "I'm never late for a good meal," she replied.

Lucy laughed. "Pour yourselves something to drink, dinner's almost ready." She lifted an oblong loaf of meat out of the pan and onto a waiting platter.

"You want a Coke?" Chris asked. He opened the fridge as he spoke.

"Sure. Uh, is there anything I can do to help?" Amber glanced toward the dining area. The table was already set. Salad and dinner rolls were sitting on the counter.

"Just take the salad and the rolls to the table," Lucy replied, "and sit yourself down."

Amber did as instructed. Lucy put the meat loaf on the table and took the chair next to Amber. Chris brought their drinks and sat down next to his grandmother.

"This looks wonderful," Amber said. "I am so hungry."

"Help yourself." Lucy smiled broadly. "We don't stand on ceremony around here." She pushed the platter toward Amber. "Dig in."

For the next few minutes they made small talk as they filled their plates. Then the conversation drifted onto other matters. Before she knew it, Amber found herself telling them about her mother.

"It was good she had you to take care of her." Lucy buttered her roll. "She was lucky. Most people have to rely on strangers when they get sick."

"Well, she did have nurses," Amber said. "I mean, I wasn't doing it on my own."

"But you did it." Chris helped himself to another slice of meat loaf. "That's really something. I don't know anyone else who's gone through something like that. I don't see how you handled it. You must really be a strong person."

"I don't think I'm any stronger than anyone else. I just did what I had to do. Besides, I didn't really have much choice," Amber said quietly. There was a lull in the conversation. She could hear the wind rattling softly against the windows.

"I'll bet you miss her, don't you," Lucy said softly.

Amber blinked hard to keep the tears back. God, yes, she missed her mother more than she could ever say. "Yeah, I do." She glanced out the window at the palm trees dancing in the evening breeze. Sometimes it was so hard to understand why God took her mother.

No one spoke for a moment, then Chris said, "Uh, is that why you don't drive? Because you were taking care of your mom?"

"There wasn't really time," Amber admitted. "By the time I was old enough to get my license, Mom's illness had taken a turn for the worse. I didn't want to take time away from her."

"And cars are expensive, too," Chris added. "I guess your cousin couldn't afford two of them."

"She wouldn't have to," Amber said. "My mom's estate would pay for a car. That's one of the things I've got to talk to Celia about. She promised me she'd talk to my lawyer and get everything arranged. You can't live in Southern California unless you drive. A girl has to have transportation."

"You're thinking of taking driving lessons?" Chris took a sip of his Coke.

"And buying a car," Amber replied. "But it's tough to talk to Celia. She's never home."

"Call the lawyer yourself," Lucy advised. She helped herself to another roll.

"Me? Call him?" That hadn't really occurred to her.

"Sure, why not? He's *your* lawyer, isn't he? If you want something done right, do it yourself. That's what I always say."

Amber stared at her as an idea blossomed in her

mind. "You're right, Lucy. If you want something done right, do it yourself. And I will."

After dinner they cleaned up and then Amber announced she had to get home. "It's a school night and I've got some homework to finish," she explained. She thanked Lucy for the great meal and then Chris walked her the few short feet to her own door.

He stared at her for a moment. In the moonlight, the angles of his face were sharp and well-defined, giving him a harsh, forbidding look. Then he smiled and he was Chris again. "You want to go out this weekend? Take in a movie or a pizza?"

"That sounds wonderful. I'd love to."

He nodded, hesitated and then leaned forward and brushed his lips across hers. "Good night. I'll call you tomorrow."

She was pleasantly startled by the brief kiss. "I'd like that. Good night."

He waited until she was safely inside before leaving. Amber sighed happily as she locked the door. The house was quiet. Celia, of course, was still out. But tonight, Amber didn't mind. She wanted these few moments to herself, wanted to savor the feeling of having someone in her life she was beginning to care about. And who, she hoped, was beginning to care about her.

She went to her bedroom and began to undress. Her top was half over her head when the phone rang. Hoping it was Chris, she made a dive for the receiver. "Hello."

"Hello, Amber." The voice was deep and male.

"Chris?"

He laughed. "In your dreams."

"Who is this?"

"Your worst nightmare." The voice dropped to a whisper.

Amber's heart beat like a jackhammer and she swallowed nervously. "Leave me alone, you creep." She might be scared, but she refused to be cowed.

"I'd be careful about calling people names," the voice hissed in an ugly whisper, "trailer park trash."

"I'm not trash," she yelled, "you are. I don't spend my free time calling strangers and trying to scare them. What's the matter, has your only friend died? Is this all you have to do? Is your life so pathetically empty and devoid of meaning that you spend your time crank-calling like an eight-year-old?"

The sharp intake of air on the other end of the line was proof that she was getting to him. "What's wrong? Cat got your tongue? Or am I using too many big words? Pathetic does have more than one syllable, but I figured even you might know what it means . . ."

"Watch your mouth, bitch," he interrupted, "or you'll really piss me off."

"Watch your mouth or you'll end up in jail. You forgot to whisper, you moron. I recognize your voice, Jack Redden."

"You'll never prove it." He sounded unsure of himself.

She plowed on, pressing her advantage. "I don't have to, the phone company will. They do keep records. Even if you were smart enough to use a pay phone, you probably went to the one nearest to your house."

"You bitch!" Redden screamed. "You'd better not show up at school tomorrow, you're really going to get it."

"So are you. Only it'll be the cops waiting for you, not that wimp of a vice principal. I'm going to call the cops. In case you didn't know it, you moron, threatening people is illegal in this state. It's called stalking."

"Do your worst, bitch," he hissed. "See if that works."

Amber was now more angry than scared. "Oh I will, you can count on that, you stupid creep."

On the other end of the line, the phone slammed down. Amber winced. She held the receiver away from her and shook her head.

He'd hung up on her.

She'd won.

But she was still scared. Despite her brave words, she knew the cops wouldn't take her seriously. Not without Celia or the school backing her up.

That wasn't going to happen. Celia didn't care and the school was too concerned about ticking off Redden's parents to do more than slap his wrists.

And tomorrow he was going to make her pay.

Amber closed her eyes. She'd have cried only she was too depressed. Oh God, why was this happening? What had she done to deserve this? What did Redden want from her? What was driving him?

She sighed. There was no point in speculating on why he'd picked her to be his victim. It was just the luck of the draw. He didn't need a reason to pick on someone. It was what Jack Redden did.

He was a bully, that's all there was to it.

Amber finished getting undressed and sank down on her bed. All around her, the night was silent. The wind had died with the sunset. Weary, she gazed blankly at the carpet. Suddenly, she heard a distinct thump from the front of the mobile home. Startled, she jumped. What on earth was that? Amber jumped off the bed and took off for the living room at a dead run.

If Redden was breaking in, she wanted to have the chance to scream her head off. Her neighbors might be old, but they all had phones and they'd call the cops in a heartbeat. Most of them had 911 on speed dial.

She skidded to a halt as the front door opened and Celia stepped inside. "What's up?" she stared at Amber curiously.

"I thought you were someone breaking in. I didn't expect you home tonight." That was a polite way of saying she assumed that Celia would spend the night at Dale's place.

She tossed her handbag on the couch. "Well, I'm here, aren't I?" she muttered, not sounding at all happy about it. "How was your day?"

Amber knew her cousin was only making conversation. Tough. She was going to get the truth. "It was fine up until a few minutes ago."

Celia yawned. "Really? What happened? No, don't tell me, let me guess. Jack Redden tried to break in . . ."

"He called me," Amber interrupted. She kept her own anger under control. Celia was acting true to form: She didn't take it seriously. Only this time, she was in for a surprise. "Actually, he threatened me."

Celia sighed. "Oh great. I suppose you want me to call the school and complain."

"You don't need to do anything. I'll take care of it myself." It was time to take matters into her own hands. Celia and the school were useless. She might as well give her own idea a shot.

"Oh really." Celia raised her eyebrows so much they almost reached her hairline. "And what are *you* planning to do?"

"What everyone else does these days. I'm going to sic my lawyer on him."

"What lawyer? What are you talking about?"

"I'm going to see Mr. Lindstrom tomorrow," Amber announced casually. "He's my attorney. Why shouldn't he help me? I'm sick and tired of being bullied. You and the school aren't doing anything to stop Redden, so I'm going to do it myself."

"But I called the school," Celia protested. "What else do you expect me to do?"

"Nothing. Like I said, I'll take care of it," she said. Her cousin was really overreacting. She hadn't expected Celia to be pleased over this new turn of events, but she hadn't expected hysterics either.

"But I can't take tomorrow off work to drive you to Orange County. Lindstrom's in Lake Forest . . ."

"I don't expect you to drive me anywhere. I'll take the train." Amber started back toward her bedroom. "It's no big deal. There's a train station at Santa Barbara. I'll get off at Irvine and take a cab the rest of the way."

"What about school?" Celia dogged her heels. "You'll miss a day."

"It'll be worth it." She opened her bedroom door and turned to face her cousin. Celia was watching her anxiously. Amber didn't understand why, but she actually looked frightened.

"This isn't a good idea." Celia bit her lip. "You'll just be wasting his time. He won't like that. Lawyers don't like seeing people without an appointment."

"I don't care whether he likes it or not," Amber replied. She didn't know why her cousin was trying so hard to stop her, but she wasn't going to give in on this. "I don't expect to see him for free. I'll make an appointment. He'll be paid."

"It's a waste of money to bother him about something this trivial," Celia cried.

"Being threatened and harassed isn't trivial!" Amber yelled. "I think it'll be worth every penny it costs me, and you know what? It's *my* money."

"I don't want you to go." Celia tried to sound stern, but couldn't quite pull it off. "I'll handle this. I'll call the school again tomorrow. I'll insist they do something."

Amber shook her head. "Nope, you had your chance, Celia. Two minutes ago you seemed to think my problem was no big deal. The good thing about sending Lindstrom in for me is even if he thinks I'm being dumb, he won't let that stop him from doing something about it. He's paid to help me."

Celia argued for another ten minutes, but Amber refused to budge.

The next morning, Amber got up, grabbed the phone and began making her calls. She got the train timetable, the bus schedule to Santa Barbara and then called Mr. Lindstrom at home.

"Hello?" The phone was answered by a woman.

"Mrs. Lindstrom?"

"Yes?"

"Hi, it's me, Amber Makepeace. I'm sorry to call so early."

"Oh, hi, Amber." Lois Lindstrom was a warm, kindly woman. She'd helped Amber make her mom's funeral arrangements. "How are you? Is everything all right?"

"I'm fine, thanks," Amber replied. "Actually, I do have a problem, that's why I'm calling so early. I wanted to know if Mr. Lindstrom could see me today."

"He's in the shower. Is this an official visit or do you want to drop by the house?"

"I'd like to see him at his office," Amber said. "It's sort of official. I'd like to make an appointment for sometime today if that's possible."

"Okay, dear, hold on and I'll go see what we can do." She put the phone down. A few minutes later, she was back. "He can see you at 1:00. Is that good for you?"

Amber mentally calculated bus and train schedules. "It's perfect. I'll be there. Nice talking to you, Mrs. Lindstrom."

"It was nice talking to you, dear."

Amber hung up and then raced for the shower. She had to make the early bus to Santa Barbara or she'd miss the train. Her schedule was tight and she wasn't going to be able to rely on anyone but herself. Celia certainly wasn't going to put herself out to help Amber make her train.

Maybe Amber would talk to Mr. Lindstom about

that situation, too. Maybe she and Celia should part company soon.

Amber made all her connections with minutes to spare. But she didn't relax until she'd made her last train change at Union Station in Los Angeles. Glancing at her watch, she sighed in relief. Barring any problems on the southbound line, she'd be at the station in Irvine by 11:30.

Amber opened the door to Mr. Lindstrom's office and stepped inside. She was ten minutes early.

"Hi, you must be Amber Makepeace," a perky, young receptionist said. She looked over the sleek, modern telephone console and smiled. "Mr. Lindstrom's expecting you." She pointed to an open doorway by her desk. "Go right through there."

"Thanks." Amber passed through the open doorway and found herself in a long hallway. She'd been here before so she knew the way. Mr. Lindstrom's office was at the end. His door was closed. She knocked softly, opened it and stepped inside.

"Hello, Amber." John Lindstrom, a tall, distinguished, silver-haired man rose from behind his massive desk and came toward her, his hand outstretched. "It's so good to see you," he said, taking the hand she offered.

"It's nice to see you, too," she replied.

"Have a seat." He motioned to the small love seat and couch on the far side of the office. "Would you like a soft drink or a cup of coffee?"

"No, thanks, I just had lunch. My train was on time so I didn't have to rush."

She took a seat on one of the overstuffed floral chairs and he plopped down on the couch and flipped open a notebook. He pulled a pen out of his pocket and smiled at her reassuringly, but she could see the concern in his eyes.

Amber took a deep breath. "I suppose you're wondering what this is all about?"

He chuckled. "You've gone to a lot of trouble to get here so I imagine that whatever it is, it's important. What's the problem?"

"I hope you won't think it's stupid, but, uh, I'm being bullied at school. No one will do anything about it."

His eyebrows drew together. "Bullied? You mean threatened?"

"That's right." Amber took another deep breath and plunged straight in. "It all started the first week of school. I've tried and tried to get Celia and the school to do something about it, but they don't seem to think it's any big deal. I can't go on like this, Mr. Lindstrom. I'm scared. That's why I came here today. You've got to help me."

"I will help you," he said calmly. His expression was all business now. "How did it start? Tell me everything and be specific."

At first, she stumbled over her words and got the time sequences wrong, but he was such a good listener, she was soon talking calmly and coherently.

When she'd finished, he stared at her for a long moment. "It doesn't sound like you've had a very nice senior year so far," he said.

Amber hesitated. She didn't want to downplay her

problems but on the other hand she didn't want him to think her life was a total disaster. "It hasn't been all bad. I've made some friends. That's how I found out about Jack's history of bullying . . ."

"History of bullying?" he repeated. "You didn't say anything about that." He checked his notes.

"Oh, I'm sorry, I didn't think it was important."

He held up his hand. "Don't apologize. Now, tell me about these other kids he's bullied and don't leave anything out, no matter how insignificant you think it might be."

Amber told him about the others. For the next hour, he bombarded her with question after question. He wanted to know all the details and about every single incident. By the time he was finished, Amber's throat was dry and she was exhausted. "I don't think I've ever talked so much," she exclaimed.

He laughed. "I like to be thoroughly prepared."

"Does that mean you can do something?" she asked eagerly. "I know this sounds crazy, but I think he's dangerous and no one, not even Celia, will do anything. I feel like I'm all alone." She hesitated.

"You're not alone," Mr. Lindstrom assured her. "I know it seems like you are, but you've always got Lois and me. You can come to us anytime and not just because I'm your lawyer. I've known you since you were born, Amber. Lois and I are very fond of you. If your mother hadn't requested that Celia be appointed your legal guardian, we'd have asked the court to appoint us."

"That's so kind of you," Amber said. She felt a little less lonely. "I guess Mom didn't want to impose on you . . ."

"Nonsense," he interrupted. "She only made that request because Celia asked her to do it."

"What? But I thought that Celia had gotten stuck with me because there was no one else." Amber didn't understand. Celia sure didn't act like she wanted a teenager living with her.

Mr. Lindstrom shook his head. "Celia asked your mom to appoint her to be your guardian. As a matter of fact, she campaigned for the job. It put Lois and I in an awkward position. We're not family so we couldn't really object."

Amber couldn't believe this. "Why would she do that? She acts like having me around is a real pain in the butt and she's never home." She was angry now. "I don't understand it. If I'd stayed with you I could have gone to El Toro and finished up my senior year with my friends. Jeez, this really stinks. I'm stuck living with a stranger and being harassed by a lunatic. It isn't fair."

"I'm sorry, Amber." Mr. Lindstrom sighed. "It doesn't seem fair. But do keep in mind that you'll be eighteen soon. If you're really unhappy in Lansdale, you can always come back here and live. You'd be welcome to stay with us or to get your own place."

Amber's outburst had drained some of her anger. "I just don't understand why she did it. I don't think she even likes me."

"She did it because of the money," Mr. Lindstrom said bluntly. "The estate pays her a generous monthly allowance to cover your living expenses. Do you have any idea how much money there was in your mother's estate?"

Amber shrugged. "Not really. Mom and I talked about finances before she died. But all she said was that there was enough to get me through college and have a bit of a nest egg."

He smiled briefly. "There's a little more than that."

"But how could there be? We weren't rich. Mom was a nurse before she got sick. Where would she get any money? I mean, I know she had an insurance policy . . ."

"Quite a large one," Mr. Lindstrom said. "As did your father. When your father died, your mother invested that money very wisely. Her policy was over a quarter of a million dollars. When you add the two together, there's almost a million dollars in trust for you."

Amber couldn't believe it. "Are you kidding?"

"Lawyers never kid about money," he replied. "You'll have access to part of that money when you turn eighteen. The rest of it will be held in trust until you're twenty-five."

It felt strange to know that she had so much money. But then again, she'd give up every penny of it if she could have either of her parents back. "Wow. Uh, I guess that means I can have driving lessons?"

"You should have already had them." He frowned. "I sent Celia a check months ago for that very purpose."

Amber snorted. "No wonder she didn't want me coming to see you." Now she understood why Celia hadn't wanted her to come here.

"I think I'd better have a chat with your guardian."
Mr. Lindstrom didn't look happy as he said, "And I
think it would be a good idea if I sent you an accounting of the estate's expenditures every quarter. Would
that be too much for you?"

"I'd like that," Amber said eagerly. "But you'd have
to help me understand all the figures and stuff."

"That's not a problem; we'll be getting together on
your eighteenth birthday to go over a number of legal
matters. I'll call you closer to that time and we'll set
something up." He leaned back in his chair. "Now, as
to your other problem, here's what I'm going to do."

It was past six by the time Amber got home. "Celia,"
she called, as she stepped inside. She tossed her purse
on the couch. "Are you here?" She was fairly sure her
cousin would be out.

"Just a sec," Celia called from inside her bedroom.
A moment later, she came into the living room. She
smiled, but Amber could see the anxiety in her eyes.
"I'm glad you're home," she said. "I was starting to
get worried."

Amber had thought about what to say to her cousin
on the long train trip back. She had plenty of reasons
to be angry and judging from the nervous smile on
Celia's face Celia knew it.

"I had a long talk with Mr. Lindstrom." Amber
plopped down on the couch. "He called the school
today and threatened them with a lawsuit unless they
do something about Jack Redden. Immediately." Actually, he'd done a bit more than that, but Amber wasn't

going to tell her cousin everything. Why should she? Celia hadn't exactly busted her tail to help.

"Uh, well, uh, I guess that's settled then," Celia replied.

"He's also going to contact Redden's parents and threaten them with a civil suit if their son doesn't leave me alone."

"Sounds like Mr. Lindstrom really took you seriously." She gave an embarrassed shrug. "I guess I shouldn't have been so casual about the whole thing. But, uh, you know, when I was in school, you just sort of had to live with this kind of stuff when it happened."

"You don't now," Amber said. "You can do something about it if you're willing to get off your butt and take action."

Celia looked away. She bit her lip. "Look, I know you think I didn't do such a hot job of being your guardian, but I did the best I could."

"The best you could?" Amber stared at her incredulously. "You've got to be kidding. You didn't do anything except buy a few more groceries and let me use you spare room."

"That's not true . . ."

"Oh, give me a break. You ignored me, you ignored my problems and you only took me in because my mom's estate paid you. Don't even deny it, Mr. Lindstrom told me everything. You wanted to become my guardian because it paid well, not because you really wanted me here. You take the checks and go on your merry way and me and my troubles can just go to hell in a . . . a . . . handbasket for all you care." She shook her head. "I cannot believe it—if you'd just stayed out of the way, I'd still be living in Lake Forest and going to my old high school. The Lindstroms wanted me. Really wanted me. I'd be living with them instead of being bullied by that lunatic Redden if it wasn't for you."

Celia's eyes filled with tears. "I'm family. I didn't do it just for the money. Okay, I'll admit it helps, but I'm your cousin. My mother and your mother were sisters. That counts for something. Do you think I like being all alone in the world? I wanted you here because you're family. All the family I've got. Just give me another chance. I'll try to do a better job. Honestly, I will."

Amber's anger died as quickly as it had flared. There was no point in yelling at her cousin. It wouldn't change anything. "You don't have to do a better job. I'll be eighteen soon and I can get my own place."

"You're not going to move out, are you?" Celia cried. "Not while you're in high school. You don't want to live on your own—it gets too lonely."

Amber raised her eyebrow.

"Okay, okay." Celia held up her hand. "I know what you're thinking. But I promise, I'll try to do better. Cut me some slack, here. I thought you'd like to have the place to yourself sometimes."

"Sometimes I would," Amber replied. "But not every night."

"I'm sorry." Celia bit her lip again. "Come on, give me another chance. I'll try to do better. How was I supposed to know how to handle a teenager? I've never had kids around before and I won't be gone all the time, honest."

"I don't want to come between you and Dale," Amber protested.

"You won't be," Celia said quickly. "We've already decided to stop seeing so much of each other. You know, give each other some space."

Amber wasn't sure what to do. She really didn't want to live by herself and Celia did have a point. She probably didn't know much about teenagers. "Okay, we can give it a try for a while longer."

Celia was visibly relieved. "You won't be sorry. Honestly. It's not just for the money. We are family. We should at least try to work things out."

"Uh, Celia, there's one more thing. Mr. Lindstrom mentioned he'd sent you money for driving lessons."

"I've already made the arrangements," Celia said. "All you need to do is decide if you want the lessons after school or on the weekends."

Chapter Nine

Dear Diary,
Tomorrow should be interesting. I know Mr. Lindstrom
called the school this afternoon and raised a ruckus.
I'll bet it really ticked Mullins off, too. More than that,
I'll bet it scared the pants off him. Too bad. If Mullins
had done his job right to begin with, he wouldn't be
getting nasty calls from my lawyer. I hope this freaks
him out so badly that he takes care of the problem and
keeps that lunatic away from me. But just in case he
doesn't, I did get a little insurance. I made a little side
trip in Los Angeles today. Even with Mr. Lindstrom
getting into the act, you never know what's going to
happen. It's better to be safe than sorry. Getting the
stuff was easy, too. The man at the liquor store didn't
ask for ID or anything. He just handed it over when I
slapped the cash on the counter. But then, it's only pep-
per spray, not mace. I feel funny carrying it, but like

Tracy said when I called her, "These days, a girl's got to rely on herself."

Amber glanced at her backpack lying on the floor by her chest of drawers. She imagined she could see the skinny outline of the spray can through the outside back pocket of the pack. Maybe she ought to tuck it into one of the side pockets, somewhere less obvious. She was fairly sure carrying pepper spray to school was against the rules. These days, everything was against the rules. The schools were so hysterical over drugs that you couldn't even carry aspirin. They'd really flip if they knew she had pepper spray.

Tough, she was taking it anyway. The school hadn't done diddly to protect her. She wasn't ever going to be defenseless again.

She slapped her diary shut and tucked it in the top drawer, reached over to the light, flipped it off and scooted down on the bed.

For the first time since the whole mess started, Amber fell asleep as soon as her head hit the pillow.

She slept like a baby.

Amber was up and out the door before Celia got out of bed. It was her cousin's late day at the hospital. She waved at Brandon as she climbed onboard her bus.

"How ya doing." He took off his sunglasses. "Were you sick yesterday?"

"No, I had to take care of something important," she replied as she swung into the seat. "I went to see my lawyer."

"No kidding!" Brandon's eyes widened. "By your-self?"

"Yup." She grinned. "He called the school and put them on notice. If they don't get Redden to back off, we'll sue."

"Man, that is so cool!" Brandon exclaimed. "You weren't just threatening old Mullins the other day? You actually did it? Jeez, I'd give anything to have been a fly on the wall in Mullins office when that call came in."

"I actually did it." Amber adjusted her backpack on her lap. "I was right there in his office when he called them. Of course Mullins was in a meeting, but I'm sure he called him back. Mr. Lindstrom, that's my lawyer, didn't beat around the bush. He told Mrs. Larchmont that if he didn't hear from Mullins we'd be filing suit against the school, the district and Mullins personally."

"I hope it scared the crap out of them," Brandon said softly. "Eric's parents were immigrants. They couldn't afford a lawyer." He snorted in disgust. "Half the time Mullins didn't even bother to return their phone calls. Man, I hope your lawyer nailed his butt good."

Amber wasn't in the least surprised by Brandon's reaction. Jack Redden had run roughshod over people for so long that even people who weren't directly bul-lied by the creep hated his guts. "Oh, I don't think Mullins will be ignoring Mr. Lindstrom's calls," she said confidently. "He's quite persistent. As a matter of fact, he even volunteered to come up here in person if he had to. Mullins doesn't want to face a lawsuit just because he was too dumb to return a phone call." She had no doubt that Mr. Lindstrom would be here in a fast minute if needed.

"Man, I can't wait for first period—there's a bunch of kids that hate Redden. They'll be so jazzed that someone finally had the guts to really do something about that jerk." He glanced at her, his expression uncertain. "Uh, I can talk about it, can't I? I mean, it doesn't have to be confidential or anything like that?"

"Feel free to tell everyone that stands still for ten seconds." Amber smiled broadly and gathered her pack. The bus pulled up to their stop and they got off.

Mr. Lindstrom hadn't said to keep the matter confidential and she was certain that if he'd wanted her to be quiet about it, he'd have told her. Besides, she'd decided that the more people who knew what was going on, the better. There was safety in numbers. Maybe if the word got around school, other kids that Redden had bullied would come forward.

She kept her eyes peeled for Redden's car as they crossed the street and went onto the campus. She didn't see him or his wheels.

Despite her resolve, for the rest of the morning Amber was constantly looking over her shoulder. By the time she went to her locker to get her history book she was so jumpy it felt like her nerve endings were on fire. She rounded the corner and stopped. But there was nothing to fear. Just a bunch of kids getting their books out of their own lockers. Redden and his creepy friend weren't waiting for her. Relieved, she got her books.

She knew she was being paranoid, but she couldn't

help it. She hadn't told Brandon everything. Mr. Lind-strom hadn't just called the school yesterday; he'd put in a call to Redden's parents as well. Even though it was what she'd wanted, now that she was here, now that she had to walk into history class and face him, she was nervous.

Redden had probably already been warned to leave her alone—surely even he wouldn't be dumb enough to keep harassing her once the lawyers got involved.

She hesitated briefly when she reached her class-room and then stepped inside. Amber stopped by the door. As usual, Mr. Powers was buried behind the news-paper and there were only a few students in the room. Jack wasn't one of them.

She sat down and waited. The passing period seemed longer than normal. The seconds and minutes dragged by as the other students ambled in and took their seats. She noticed that several of them were star-ing at her curiously. Apparently, Brandon was spread-ing the word. She kept waiting for Jack. But every time she turned and looked at the back of the class, his desk remained empty. Finally, the bell rang and Mr. Powers put the sports section down.

"I hope you all did your reading assignments for this week," Mr. Powers said. He picked up a stack of papers off the corner of his desk.

Everyone groaned.

"You guessed it." He laughed and handed the stack of papers to Amber. "It's pop quiz time."

"The Padres lose again?" someone asked from the back of the class. "You always give a quiz when that team bites the dust."

Everyone, even Powers, laughed. "It's not always the Padres," he shot back, "sometimes I do it when the Mets lose."

Amber took her quiz and passed them on. As she swung around to the front, Julie Steadman walked into the room. It was the first time she'd been in class since the day she'd turned tail and run.

The laughter died and the room went silent. Everyone stared at Julie as she crossed the room to Mr. Powers.

"Thanks, Julie," he instructed as he continued passing the quiz out, "just put your readmit on my desk and sit down."

"Okay," Julie replied. She tossed it onto the desk and hurried to her seat.

Amber stared at her. Julie glanced at the teacher, saw that he was talking to Hector Jameison and then leaned across the aisle. "I've got to talk to you," she whispered. "Wait for me after class."

Amber hesitated; she wasn't sure she trusted Julie. "Well, okay."

"All right, class." Mr. Powers stepped to the front of the room and picked up the sports section. "You've got twenty minutes."

The moment class was over, the two girls went outside. "What do you want?" Amber asked as soon as they were out the door.

"Let's go over there." Julie pointed to a shady spot near the fence, away from the classrooms and walkways. "I want some privacy."

More curious than alarmed, Amber followed the tall

blonde across the grass. They stopped under a tree. "Okay, what is it?"

Julie looked grim. "First of all, I want to apologize. I did change your answers on that quiz. I'm really sorry, too."

"Why? Why'd you do it?"

"Because I was dumb." Julie sighed. "I was ticked off that you'd taken John's seat. I like John . . . heck, the whole school knows I've had a crush on him since tenth grade."

"You changed my paper because you had a crush on John Berry?" Amber shook her head in disgust. "Someone actually told me that was probably the reason, but I didn't believe him. I couldn't believe anyone was that stupid."

"I know, I know," Julie said quickly. "It was stupid, I'll admit that. But that wasn't the only reason I did it, honestly. I've got to make you understand."

"Why?" Amber asked. "You've told me what happened. I'm not going to do anything. I'm not going to snitch you out to Powers. My grades can take one bad quiz."

"You don't understand," she wailed. "If you don't help me, I'll be kicked off the cheerleaders squad and tossed out of school. You've got to go to Mr. Mullins's office. You've got to tell him that you're not mad anymore and that you accepted my apology."

"What are you talking about . . ." Amber's voice trailed off as she realized what must have happened. "Oh no, I told my lawyer about how you changed my paper and that I thought this guy who's been harassing me put you up to it . . ."

"Jack Redden did put me up to it," Julie interrupted. Her expression was frantic. "He gave me fifty bucks to change your answers."

"Fifty bucks! Are you kidding?"

"I wish I was." Julie moaned softly. "I know it was wrong. I know I shouldn't have done it, but Jack scares me. I was afraid to say no. I was scared he'd start picking on me instead of you. Please, please help me. If you don't tell Mullins you've forgiven me, he'll kick me out of school."

"How does Mullins know what happened?" Amber asked. "Like I told my lawyer, it's my word against yours. If you said you hadn't changed my answers, I couldn't prove you did. A few eraser marks on a paper isn't exactly evidence that you were the one with the pencil. It could just as easily be me changing my answers before we switched papers."

"I got called into the office this morning," Julie replied. She swallowed nervously. "Mullins asked me about the quiz and I got so rattled I told him everything. He's going to kick me out. I just know it. You've got to help me. For God's sake, *you* should understand how scary Jack can be."

Amber hesitated. She did understand. But she wasn't sure if she should say anything to the vice principal now. The whole mess was in the hands of her lawyer. "Gee, I don't know. My lawyer's gotten involved now . . ."

"All you have to do is talk to Mullins." Julie's eyes filled with tears.

Amber sighed. "All right, I'll do what I can."

"Amber Makepeace."

She whirled around as her name was called. Mr. Powers stood at the edge of the walkway. She glanced at Julie as she started across the grass. "Don't worry, I'll try to get Mullins to lay off."

"Thanks," Julie said gratefully.

"You're wanted in Mr. Mullins's office," Mr. Powers told her as she approached. He looked frankly curious.

She nodded. "I'll go right away." She could feel his stare as she hurried toward the administration building.

Amber's heart raced as she went through the double doors and headed down the hall. Jeez, she didn't want to do this. She'd much rather face the vice principal with Mr. Lindstrom here. Why was Mullins calling her in now? Was he going to try to make her back down? By the time she reached the office door, her stomach was in knots and her knees were shaking. Get a grip, she told herself. She closed her eyes and forced a long, slow breath into her lungs and stepped inside.

Dragon Lady, Mrs. Larchmont, leapt to her feet as soon as she spotted Amber. She plastered a fake smile on her face. "Hello, dear. Mr. Mullins is waiting for you. Go right on in."

Dear? Give me a break, Amber thought. Two days ago, this woman wouldn't give her the time of day. But she was too polite to ignore Mrs. Larchmont. "Thank you," she mumbled.

Mullins was on the phone when she walked into his office. "She's here now," he said into the mouthpiece. "Yes, yes, I'll call you back as soon as I've spoken with her." He put the phone down and smiled briefly.

"Hello, Amber. Sit down. It looks like we've got a bit of a problem."

Amber wasn't nervous anymore, now she was annoyed. She had a feeling she knew what was coming. They were either going to try to sweet-talk her into calling off Mr. Lindstrom or they were going to try intimidation. She looked Mullins dead in the eyes as she sat down. "I don't have a problem," she said flatly. "Not anymore."

Mullins lips flattened into a thin line that he twisted into a dumb smile. "Now, now, now, don't you think you've gone a bit too far? There's been a terrible misunderstanding here. I assure you, had we known how frightened you were here, we'd have been a tad more assertive in handling the problem."

She couldn't believe her ears. "You've got to be kidding. I came in here twice to try to get something done about that maniac and both times you acted like I was some kind of mental case."

A dark red flush crept up the vice principal's face. "Apparently, you misunderstood me," he began.

"I didn't misunderstand anything," she interrupted. "Nor did my legal guardian. Remember, she called you as well. You didn't do anything."

"I most certainly did," he snapped. He took a deep breath, flashed her a fake smile and brought himself under control. "I called Jack Redden in here and told him in the strongest terms to leave you alone."

"Yeah, you really gave it to him, didn't you?"

"Based on the evidence we had at the time, it was all I could do," Mullins shot back. She could tell he was struggling to keep a lid on his temper. He was either very scared or very ticked off. Amber didn't really care which. This was the man that had let lots of other kids suffer because he didn't want to take on the Reddens. Now he was sweating his job. Good.

"You could have done lots more," she accused. "You could have gotten that creepy friend of his in here and made him tell the truth. You could have found out which one of those kids out there"—she jerked her head toward the outer office—"was working in here the day Jack got my locker combination. You could have talked to some of the kids that had run-ins with Redden before and gotten their statements. But you didn't do any of that, did you?" Amber paused for breath. She knew she ought to shut up. Mullins was turning purple in fury and she ought to get out of there before she got suspended herself. But she couldn't stop herself. All the fear and the anger and the rage of the past weeks came pouring out. "Tell me, Mr. Mullins, exactly what did you say to him? Did you take notes, did you write him up for disciplinary action, is there a written warning in his file? Or did you just slap his wrists like all the other times?"

Mullins's eyes bulged. "How dare you speak to me like that," he finally gasped. "How dare you?" He got up and leaned across his desk, glaring at her. "Who do you think you are? You kids have no respect . . ."

"Mr. Mullins. What's going on here?" A woman's voice cut through the vice principal's tirade.

Mullins looked stricken. "Mrs. Reed. What are you doing here? You're supposed to be at a conference in San Francisco."

"I flew back early this morning when I heard that

one of our students was filing a hazing suit against us."
She frowned and crossed her arms over her chest.
"Luckily, my secretary was able to get hold of me before I left the hotel room. You really should have
called me when you heard from Miss Makepeace's
lawyer yesterday." She turned her attention to Amber.
"I assume you're Amber Makepeace."

"That's right."

"Uh, I was just trying to explain to Amber that we
have procedures here . . ." Mullins began.

"He was yelling at me because I told the truth,"
Amber interrupted. She stared at the tall, silver-haired
superintendent. "I apologize for losing my own temper. But I don't appreciate being called in here and intimidated because I'm exercising my legal rights."

"That wasn't what I was doing," Mullins protested.

"That's what it felt like to me," Amber said.

"I'll take over from here," Mrs. Reed said.

"But I assure you," Mullins sputtered. "There's no
need for you to intervene, I've got the situation well in
hand. I've put a call into the Reddens."

Mrs. Reed waved him off. "I canceled your call.
I've already seen the Reddens and taken care of everything."

"But how could that be? You've only just arrived . . ."

"The Redden family met me at the district office in
Santa Barbara at ten this morning and my secretary got
me copies of Julie Steadman's statement." She turned
her attention to Amber. "Come with me." She headed
across the short hall to Mr. Dankers's office. Amber
follower her.

The superintendent closed the door as soon as they were inside.

"Please sit down," Mrs. Reed instructed. She nodded toward one of the two chairs in front of the desk.

Amber sat down.

Mrs. Reed took a seat behind the desk. She sighed and shook her head. "This isn't the kind of situation we like in our school system."

Amber swallowed. She was tired and to be perfectly honest, a little bit scared. But she wasn't going to back down. Not now. She'd gone too far. "Then the school administration should have taken care of the problem when it was first brought to their attention."

"I agree." Mrs. Reed smiled. "Had I known that you were being harassed, I would have done something about it. But Mr. Mullins generally handles disciplinary matters. Now, what can we do about this current situation? First of all, I'd like you to know that Jack Redden won't be coming back to Lansdale High."

"He won't?" She was shocked. "You mean, he's been expelled?"

"Not exactly." Mrs. Reed shook her head. "Your accusations and Julie Steadman's statement, coupled with Jack's past history, gave us enough evidence to expel him. But Jack's parents didn't want an expulsion on his record. They agreed to withdraw him from school."

"Julie was scared of Jack," Amber said. "Just like everyone else." She frowned. "Past history? I don't understand. You're admitting you knew he bullied kids . . ."

"I'm admitting nothing," she said calmly. "I'm

merely stating that there were a number of previous complaints about Jack in his school record. Mr. and Mrs. Redden decided of their own accord to pull him out of school when faced with a potential lawsuit and the fact that previous accusations against their son might come up in any legal proceeding."

"I'm not going to sue," Amber said bluntly. "If he's gone I'll call off my lawyer. But I'll never understand why he was allowed to stay in this school, why he got away with hurting so many kids."

"I haven't got an answer to that." Mrs. Reed smiled sadly. "Had I been principal here, he wouldn't have gotten away with it. I assure you. Can I tell the Board of Education you're dropping your lawsuit?"

"Yes. I'm sorry it had to come to this, but uh, I was kind of desperate."

Mrs. Reed laughed. "The next time you get desperate, come see me. Okay? I suspect my listening skills are a bit better than those of Mr. Mullins."

Amber got up. "Uh, there's just one more thing."

"What?"

"It's about Julie Steadman . . ."

"Don't worry about her—she admitted changing your quiz paper." Mrs. Reed reached for the phone. "She'll be suspended."

"But that's just it," Amber protested. "I don't think she should be."

"But she cheated," Mrs. Reed pointed out. "Under the district guidelines, that's considered cheating. We really don't have a choice . . ."

"But she was doing it under duress." Amber racked her brain for some legalese to throw out. She wished she could remember more of the dialogue from those old *Perry Mason* reruns she used to watch with her mom. "There were extenuating circumstances. Jack Redden threatened her. Doesn't that make her one of his victims?"

"I don't understand why you're defending her." Mrs. Reed put down the phone.

"I'm defending her because I understand what she was going through. She was scared. Scared of him."

Mrs. Reed drummed her fingers on the desktop and cocked her head to one side. "Hmmm, I guess you could make a case for her being one of his victims."

Amber silently prayed that Julie had kept her mouth shut about taking the fifty bucks from Redden. "I think she was a victim. Just like me."

Mrs. Reed said nothing. "All right," she finally said. "I'm not going to suspend her."

"Thanks, Mrs. Reed, I'm sure she'll never do anything like that again."

"She's lucky, Amber. You're a decent girl. Most people wouldn't go out of their way to help someone who'd tried to harm them." She pulled open the top drawer and took out a pad of paper. She scribbled something, tore off the top sheet and handed it across the desk. "Here, this is a readmit. We've taken up most of your lunchtime. Go and eat. If you're late to your next class, use the readmit."

"Thanks, Mrs. Reed." Amber got up and took the paper. "I appreciate all you've done."

"No problem, that's what I'm here for." She smiled kindly. "Believe it or not, there are school administrators who actually care about the well-being of their students."

"I'm sure there are," Amber agreed. She left the office. As she passed Dragon Lady's desk, Mrs. Larchmont gazed at her coldly, but said nothing. Mr. Mullins's office was empty.

Amber went out into the empty hallway. She glanced at her watch. There was ten minutes of lunch left. If she got a move on, she could get to her lunch spot by the library before the next bell. Hopefully, her friends would still be there. She flew down the hall and out to the quad. She couldn't wait to see Harriet, Brandon and Mark. She wanted to tell them everything. Especially Brandon. Jack Redden was finished at this school. Absolutely finished. He was never going to bully anyone again.

For once, the good guys had won.

Chapter
Ten

Dear Diary,
This has got to be one of the weirdest moments of my
life. All of my friends were really jazzed about getting
rid of Redden, but I feel kind of funny about the whole
thing. When I walked away from Mrs. Reed yesterday,
I was so happy I wanted to flip cartwheels across the
quad—and I couldn't wait to tell Harriet, Mark and
Brandon that I'd won. But you know what? I didn't win
anything. All I did was send a creepy kid to some other
school where he'll make some other poor kid's life
miserable. After I thought about the whole lousy deal,
I decided it sucks. Jack Redden isn't going to change
and neither are his rich parents. He'll go right on
through life picking on kids who can't fight back and
the Reddens will be right behind him, cleaning up his
mess. A real victory would have been getting Jacky
boy in therapy and making his parents agree to keep

*their checkbook shut. Oh well, it makes me sad, but at
least he's out of my life. I just hope his next victim is
someone like me, someone who'll fight back. But like
Brandon pointed out, I had a few tricks up my sleeve
that most kids don't have: money and a lawyer.*

"Hey, you almost ready in there?" Celia rapped
lightly on the door. "I just saw Chris pull up."

"Already?" Amber tossed her diary to one side and
leapt off the bed. "I'll be right out."

She glanced at her watch and saw that he was a few
minutes early for their date. But she didn't panic. She
was almost ready and she was certain he'd pop in to
say hello to Lucy before he came to pick her up.

Amber took a look at herself in the mirror, decided
the blue tank top, form-fitting jeans and white sandals
looked just right for a casual date. She grabbed her little purse off the top of her dresser and headed out to
the living room.

Celia looked up from the crossword puzzle she was
working on and nodded approvingly. "You look good,
kid. Where are you two going?"

"To the movies," Amber replied. "We'll probably
grab a burger or something afterward."

"What time do you think you'll be home?"

Amber was a bit surprised. But after what had happened between them, she wasn't going to argue with
Celia for acting like a guardian. She grinned. "I don't
know, what's my curfew?"

Celia's brows came together as she considered
the question. "Gosh, I don't know . . . you're a senior . . . What kind of curfews do the other kids have?

Oh gosh, this is silly. You're a lot more mature than I was when I was your age. Let's do it this way: If you're going to be out past midnight, you'll call. Okay?"

"Sounds good to me."

There was a knock on the door.

"That's Chris," Amber said as she opened up. "Hi."

"Hi. You ready?"

She waved good-bye to Celia. "I'll call if I'm going to be late."

Chris led her to a white Buick and unlocked the passenger door. "It was so hot, my mom let me use her car. My air-conditioning doesn't work very well."

"That was nice of her." Amber slid inside. As soon as Chris got in behind the wheel, she said, "I've got my first driving lesson tomorrow."

"Thanks for the warning." He put the key in the ignition and started the engine. "I'll be sure to stay off the roads."

She slapped him playfully on the arm. "Hey, I'm going to be a good driver. But I am a little nervous."

Chris laughed. "So am I."

"Very funny."

"Just kidding. You'll do great." He pulled out and drove slowly down the small street between the mobile homes. "What do you feel like seeing tonight?"

"Well, actually . . ." Amber hesitated. This was their first real date and she didn't want to be pushy. On the other hand, she didn't want to be one of those wimpy girls who had no ideas or opinions of their own. No guy, not even one as neat as Chris was worth that. "Uh, there's on old science fiction movie playing at that theatre downtown."

"Forbidden Planet!"

"That's it," Amber replied. "I've been dying to see it."

"Me, too." He grinned from ear to ear. "Man, have you been talking to my grandma? I've been wanting to see that since it started showing there . . . I just haven't had time."

"I love science fiction," she said. "I've got a whole list of old movies I'm trying to track down."

"Have you ever seen *Predator*?"

"That's a good one," she agreed. They talked non-stop all the way downtown.

After the movie was over, Chris grabbed Amber's hand as they left the theatre. "What'd you think of it?"

"Loved it," she said enthusiastically. "Even the special effects weren't too bad . . ."

"I know what you mean," he said as they went out into the lobby. "Sometimes with these old flicks the effects are really bad. You want to go to Harbingers and grab a burger?"

"That sounds great. I'm starved."

"You should have had some popcorn," he said.

The warm California air washed over them as they stepped outside. They walked the few blocks to the popular burger joint and went inside. Just as Amber suspected, the place was crowded with kids from Lansdale High and the local junior college. Two or three people called to Chris.

"Hey, Chris, long time no see," a tall, lanky kid yelled from behind the counter.

"Hi, Tom." Chris waved.

"There's a booth open." He pointed to a spot halfway down the diner. A busboy was just finishing up. "Grab it quick. It looks like the movies have just let out."

"Thanks, Tom." Chris grabbed her hand and pulled her toward the booth. Amber saw a lot of kids that she recognized. Some of their mouths gaped open when they saw who she was with. She couldn't stop herself from feeling just a bit smug. It was cool to be seen with someone like Chris. "You know a lot of people," she said as they slid into the booth.

He shrugged. "I've lived here all my life." He grabbed a menu from the holder and handed it to her. "And I played football. I guess that made me kind of popular."

"Kind of popular," she repeated incredulously. "You've got to be kidding. When I first mentioned your name to my friends they knew who you were and they'd never even been to a football game. As a matter of fact, Harriet said you were a BMOC . . ."

"Big Man on Campus . . . Oh my God." He laughed and held up his hand. "Come on, you're embarrassing me. You're not exactly a troll yourself . . ."

"Hey, you guys, can we join you?" Mark, dragging a sheepish Harriet in his wake, hurried toward them. "We're starved and there aren't any tables."

"Feel free." Chris slid over to the far end. "You don't mind, do you?" he asked Amber. At her nod, he patted the spot next to him. "Why don't you slide over here next to me so Harriet and Mark can have that side?"

It took a few minutes to get them all arranged. Then the waitress came and took their orders. They all had the same thing, burgers and fries.

"I'm sorry for barging in on you," Harriet said as soon as the waitress had gone.

"You didn't barge in on us," Chris said quickly. "It's nice to see you again. I enjoyed that evening at your place. What have you been doing tonight? Amber and I went to see *Forbidden Planet* at the Roxy."

Amber was so proud of him. He really was a fabulous guy. He could easily have made Mark and Harriet feel uncomfortable. "It was good, too," she added.

"Believe it or not, we went to a play with my parents." Harriet rolled her eyes. "They dragged us to the little theatre over by the library."

"Hey, it wasn't that bad," Mark said. "I liked the play."

"Are you kidding?" Harriet shook her head. "You're just being nice, Mark. But let's face it, that play was one of the most boring things ever written." She looked at Chris and Amber. "It was one of those stupid experimental plays. No plot, no story, just dumb monologues by bad actors dressed in black, ranting about how miserable the world is. Even my parents didn't like it."

"Okay, so it wasn't all that great." Mark grinned. "Let's face it, the real reason we did this number with them was so they could get a look at the guy that's dating their daughter." He looked at Harriet, his expression serious. "Do you think they liked me?"

Harriet have him a dreamy smile. "Of course they

liked you. Otherwise, they'd have found some excuse for dragging me home with them."

"Cool." He sighed in relief. "Dating. Jeez, it's enough to bring a strong man to his knees." He grinned at Amber. "You must be feeling good. Man, everyone is talking about what you did. Half the school hated Redden, they were practically cheering in Auto Shop when the word got around—" He broke off as he saw the expressions on Amber's and Chris's faces.

"What are you talking about?" Chris asked. He spoke to Mark, but he was staring at Amber.

"Oops," Harriet mumbled. "I think you've just stuck your foot in it, Mark."

"What's going on here?" Chris paused as the waitress brought their drinks.

As soon as she'd gone, Amber said, "There's something I guess I should tell you. I, uh, had a problem with a kid at school."

"Jack Redden?" Chris asked.

She nodded. "Yeah. He tried to bully me . . ."

"Why didn't you tell me!" Chris exclaimed. "That guy's a bastard. If I'd known he was giving you trouble, I'd have straightened him out in two seconds flat."

"It's okay now," she said quickly. "He won't bother me again."

"He won't bother anyone," Harriet added. "After Amber sicced her lawyer on him, his parents pulled him out of school. I hear he's going to St. Anthony's over in Santa Barbara."

Chris stared at Amber. "Why don't you tell me exactly what happened? Take it from the top and don't leave anything out."

The three of them told Chris the whole story as they ate their food. Mark did most of the talking.

Amber watched Chris carefully. By the time they got to the end of the tale, she had the feeling that Chris wasn't happy. She suspected she knew why.

But Chris was a perfect gentleman. He didn't say anything to make Harriet or Mark feel uncomfortable. He didn't even bring the subject up until they were driving back to the mobile home park.

"Why didn't you tell me what that jerk was doing to you?" he asked softly.

"I didn't want you to think I was a geeky loser," she answered honestly.

He pulled up in front of Lucy's. "Geeky loser?" he repeated. "Why would I think that? God, Amber, did you think I was that shallow?"

"No, that's not what I thought at all," she protested.

"Then you should have told me what was going on," he insisted. "For crying out loud, we're dating. Now I find out that you were being bullied by that guy and you didn't even bother to tell me. Everyone at school knew about it, but I didn't."

"It wasn't like that," she insisted. "I didn't know what to do. Give me a break here—I've never had a boyfriend. I'm just now learning the rules about dating. I don't know how much of my life to share . . . Oh gosh, I didn't know if you'd want to be involved! Getting bullied sounds so pathetic. I didn't know what to do. I almost told you."

"I wish you had." He sighed. "Next time, tell me what's going on, okay?"

Next time? Amber thought that sounded hopeful. "Okay, I promise. The next time someone picks on me, you'll be the first to know."

"Good." Chris leaned across and pulled her into his arms. "I won't let anyone hurt you, Amber. You can count on that."

He kissed her.

Just then the lights came on at Lucy's and at Celia's. A second later, Lucy stuck her head out her front door. "Is that you, Chris?"

Reluctantly, he pulled away. "Come on, I'll walk you to your door."

The next morning, Amber took her first driving lesson. She did pretty well, but she was relieved when her instructor dropped her off at home.

"How'd it go?" Celia asked. She was sitting at the kitchen table, working on another crossword puzzle.

Amber got a soft drink from the fridge. "It was kind of nerve-wracking," she admitted. "But I think I did all right. I didn't hit anything."

"What's the teacher like?" Celia asked.

"She's real nice." Amber sat down across from her cousin. "Very patient and she's got nerves of steel, too."

"That's a requirement for being a driving teacher." Celia grinned. "Oh, by the way, Chris called. He wants you to meet him at Medlow Park this evening."

"Really?" Amber frowned. Medlow Park was all the way downtown, next to Lansdale High. "He wants me to meet him at the park? That's weird. He told me he had to do something with his parents tonight and that we couldn't see each other until tomorrow."

"Plans change." Celia shrugged. "Don't worry, I'll give you a lift to the park. I'm meeting Dale tonight for dinner . . ." She broke off and looked at Amber hesitantly.

"You have a right to a life," Amber said quickly. "I don't expect you to give up seeing Dale. I appreciate the effort you've made to be home more often, but I don't expect you to be here every minute."

Celia looked relieved. "All right. So how about it? You want a ride tonight?"

"Sure. I guess Chris can bring me home."

"He'd better," Celia said. "Or he'll answer to me."

Amber spent the rest of the day doing chores, homework and fretting over what to wear. She finally settled on jeans and a tank top. As she was scrambling around in her closet, looking for her shoes, she accidentally kicked the can of pepper spray and it went rolling into the center of her room.

"You about ready?" Celia asked. She stuck her head in the room.

Amber, not wanting to go through a lot of explanations about how and why she had pepper spray, snatched up the small cannister and tucked it in her back pocket. "I'm ready."

"Good, let's get a move on then. Dale's already at the restaurant."

She dropped Amber off at the park. "Call home if you're going to be late," she instructed. "I'll be home about eleven."

"Okay." Amber waved good-bye and then went into the park. Medlow Park was an old one, filled with big leafy trees, heavy shrubbery and lush green grass. It covered several acres. Amber stopped and looked around. The place was deserted. She didn't see Chris anywhere. Then she spotted a guy in a white baseball cap sitting on a bench at the play area on the far side of the baseball diamond.

His back was to her, but she was fairly sure it was Chris. She recognized the cap. She started up the dirt path and grimaced as she realized the ground was wet. They must have watered.

The path twisted and turned through a grove of trees and Amber felt a bit apprehensive as she went farther into the park. The heavy brush and the over-hanging branches made the place look spooky. She picked up her pace, wanting to get out of the trees and back into the open.

Jack Redden stepped out from behind a tree. She stopped and backed up.

He gave her an ugly smile. "Surprised to see me?"

"Leave me alone." Keeping her eyes on him, she began to back up.

"I'll leave you alone," he sneered, "as soon as I've taught you a lesson. Did you think I'd let you get away with ruining my life, bitch?"

"I didn't ruin your life." She kept on moving back-ward. "You did. Now if you'll just leave me alone, we can forget we ever had this conversation and you won't end up in jail."

"I'm not forgetting anything," he snarled. "And I'll risk jail if it means I can put you in the hospital."

He lunged for her.

Amber turned and ran for her life. She opened her mouth and screamed.

She could hear his footsteps pounding behind her. She leapt off the path and onto the grass, trying desperately to get back to the street side of the park before he got her.

"Shut up," he yelled.

But Amber kept right on screaming. Her legs hurt and her lungs burned as she raced through the trees, heading for the open grass. Suddenly, she was jerked back. She fell hard on her butt.

Redden, his face a mask of rage, bore down on her. She kicked out at him and scrambled to one side, pulling out the can of spray as she regained her feet.

He grabbed her arm and whirled her around. Amber had a grip on the can. As they came face-to-face, she lifted her arm and pressed the button.

He howled in pain as the stream of spray got him square in the face. "You bitch," he screamed. "You've blinded me." He let go of her, dropped to his knees and frantically rubbed his eyes.

She whirled around, intending to make another run for the street. To her relief, she saw two cops running toward them. "He attacked me," she gasped, pointing at Redden.

"We saw the whole thing," one of the policemen sand as they rushed past her. The cop pushed Redden onto his stomach, twisted his arms behind his back and cuffed him.

The other policeman, seeing his partner had things

under control, came back to Amber. "Are you all right, miss? Did he hurt you?"

"No, I used pepper spray on him and got away. But thank goodness you came along when you did . . ."

"We patrol here every evening," the policeman said. "There's been some trouble with vandals. Do you know who this guy is?" He pointed to Redden as the other policeman hauled him to his feet.

"His name is Jack Redden. He's been stalking me." She took a deep, calming breath.

"Stalking you?"

She shook her head. "He lured me here by pretending to be my boyfriend. He lured me here to hurt me."

"What's your name, miss?" The officer's expression was grim.

"Amber Makepeace."

"You'd better come down to the station with us, Miss Makepeace. We'll need a statement from you. Stalking is a very serious offense."

"I know," she said. "I'll come with you. I've got quite a story to tell." She stared at Redden as the police officer lead him off across the grass. He looked at her as he went past. There was a panicked, almost frightened expression in his eyes. He'd gone too far this time.

And Amber was going to make sure that he went to jail.

Dear Diary,
It's been quite a day, let me tell you. It seemed like it took hours down at the police station. I called Celia as soon as we got there and she came right away. But

even with her there, it was a weird experience. I mean, how often do you have to give a statement to the cops!

They had me talk to a detective. I started at the beginning and told him everything. He took even more notes than Mr. Lindstrom. Celia put in a call to Lindstrom, too. He wanted to come up but I told him it wasn't necessary. The police believed me. As Detective Severs said, "There's plenty of corroborating evidence." Anyway, to make a long story short, Jack is in jail. I don't know how long he'll stay there—I'm sure his parents will whip out their checkbook and bail him out pretty quick, but for the moment, he's definitely not going to be coming around here.

I asked Detective Severs what was likely to happen to Jack. Severs didn't know. He said that as it was Jack's first offense, there was a good chance he wouldn't do any real prison time. But now that he's been arrested, he'll probably leave me alone. He said that Jack was scared to death when he was booked. Good. I hope he stays that way.

Of course, I got the usual lecture about how dangerous pepper spray is and all that. But you know what, I'm glad I had it. What if the police hadn't shown up? What if I'd had to make it out of that park on my own? Celia yammered at me all the way home about it, too. So I told her I wouldn't buy any more of the stuff.

I had my fingers crossed when I said it, though.

I don't care what anyone says. If I've learned one thing, I've learned that when push comes to shove, the only person in this old world you can really rely on is yourself.

This, of course, is a thought I won't be sharing with Chris. I called him. He's on his way over now. He's a wonderful person and if he'd have been in the park this evening, he'd have protected me. But the truth is, sometimes you're all alone. Sometimes your family, friends and boyfriend aren't around. Sometimes, you've got to rely on yourself.

National Bestselling Authors of *Sunset Island*
CHERIE BENNETT and
JEFF GOTTESFELD

University
HOSPITAL

Five young men and women follow their
hearts—and challenge their dreams—in the
life-or-death world of medicine.

__0-425-17144-2/$4.50

University Hospital: Condition Critical
__0-425-17256-2/$4.50

University Hospital: Crisis Point
__0-425-17338-0/$4.50